Penny's jaw dropped

Ryan couldn't deny enjoying her stunned expression as he stood before her, dangling a pair of heart-shaped handcuffs covered in red velvet.

"That was a-a gag gift—" she gesticulated wildly "—for my twenty-fifth birthday."

"Twenty-fifth, huh? How long ago was that?"

"Almost four years."

"Keeping them handy for some reason?"

She continued to look mortified, and Ryan mischievously took pleasure from it.

"Okay, fine, you caught me. I was cleaning out the basement and found them. I guess I was sort of saving them just in case...."

He shook his head as he dropped the handcuffs on the bed and came toward her. Although it had been fun for a minute, he didn't want her to be so embarrassed about a side of her that was so fun, so enticing. "Penny, I like it. And I really don't mind."

"Don't mind what?" she asked, exasperated.

He winked and pulled her into a warm embrace. "Trying the cuffs out later."

Dear Reader,

When my editor at Harlequin invited me to write a book for Temptation's WRONG BED miniseries, I wanted to do something really sexy and really fun. The result is *Something Wild*.

Of course, when I sat down to write a book about sexual fantasy, the last thing I expected was to also end up writing a book about a woman's struggle to reconcile her sexual self with the "good girl" the rest of the world saw. My heroine, Penny, became a lot more complex than I originally anticipated and I enjoyed exploring the various layers of her personality. Ryan's character, too, held surprises for me as I wrote, but he still turned out to be the perfect guy to help Penny live out her fantasies.

I hope you'll enjoy the roller-coaster ride of Penny and Ryan's relationship and that you'll feel their story lives up to its title!

Happy reading!

Toni Blake

P.S. Visit me online at toniblake.com.

Books by Toni Blake

HARLEQUIN TEMPTATION
800—HOTBED HONEY
825—SEDUCING SUMMER

SOMETHING WILD
Toni Blake

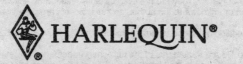
HARLEQUIN®

TORONTO • NEW YORK • LONDON
AMSTERDAM • PARIS • SYDNEY • HAMBURG
STOCKHOLM • ATHENS • TOKYO • MILAN • MADRID
PRAGUE • WARSAW • BUDAPEST • AUCKLAND

To Robin—
my best friend since the seventh grade
my companion and confidante
my almost sister

ISBN 0-373-25970-0

SOMETHING WILD

Copyright © 2002 by Toni Herzog.

Visit us at www.eHarlequin.com

Printed In U.S.A.

1

Meet me tonight. Ten o'clock. Corner of Fourth and Walnut.

And be ready for anything.

Penny

PENNY HALLORAN released a nervous sigh as she peered down at the note she'd just penned on a plain white card bearing her business's logo. She wished she'd had something more romantic to write on, perhaps scented stationery, something with flowers or hearts. Or maybe something sexier than that—animal print came to mind, then leather, then lace—but she doubted stationery had made such leaps yet. She read the words once more and wrinkled up her nose. What she'd written them on was irrelevant. What mattered was, could she go through with this?

She wasn't usually an impulsive woman, and if her plan could wait, she'd let it. This was the sort of thing that needed weeks of preparation to make sure it came off without a hitch. Even the note seemed lackluster; she wished she'd had time to think of something more clever, playful. But it *couldn't* wait—Martin was going out of town tomorrow, and when he returned in a week, he expected an answer to his marriage proposal. Tonight was the night for action.

Swallowing her fears, Penny reached for a stapler and attached the card to the bag containing Martin's sandwich—ham and Swiss on rye, light mayo—the same kind he ordered every day. Then she gathered the bag lunches that had to be delivered to Schuster Software Systems upstairs. "Be back in five," she said to her sister, Patti, who stood working the bar of the Two Sisters Restaurant and Pub as the lunch hour started. Exiting the restaurant into the building's lobby, she headed for the elevator.

This is really quite simple, she lectured herself as the elevator climbed toward the eighth floor of the downtown Cincinnati office building. *I'm just going to seduce him, that's all. Nothing to be nervous about. Men love this sort of thing,* or so she'd heard. *Martin will love it, too.* And as for why her heart was beating ninety miles an hour and her stomach felt as if it had been left back on the ground floor...well, that was only because she'd never seduced a man before. And maybe it was also because Martin's expressions of affection so far had been...less than enthusiastic. Good-night kisses at the door that often felt more obligatory than passionate. And hand-holding, Martin was big on hand-holding. But nothing more.

Oddly, that hadn't bothered Penny in the three months they'd been dating. Martin was everything she wanted in a man—ambitious, dependable, sensible and smart. Tall and lean with trim brown hair that never touched his collar, he was even somewhat handsome in a simple yet classic way. On top of that, he owned his own company, so they shared an entrepreneurial spirit, too. And at twenty-eight, Penny was mature enough to know there was more to life than sex. She enjoyed his companionship; they liked the same movies and had the same tastes in restaurants, and they loved spending lazy weekend afternoons picnicking at Eden Park, then meandering through the art museum afterward.

A few days ago, however, Martin had taken her hand in his and said, "Penny, I'm in my thirties now, and I want children before I'm too old to enjoy them. I think you and I make a good team. Will you marry me?" It had been an unexpected turn of events, all things considered. And although it hadn't been the most romantic proposal in the world, Penny couldn't deny that Martin was right. They made a good team; they were well-suited. Still, it was only now, with a marriage proposal on the table, that she'd come to realize sex *was* important, and she just didn't think she could marry him without...taking a test drive, so to speak.

In fact, in the three long days since Martin's proposal, Penny had done a lot of long, hard and rather *disturbing* thinking about herself. Disturbing because, not only did sex matter to her, and not only did it suddenly matter a lot, it was also beginning to matter in ways she'd never even imagined before.

After several stops to let other passengers on and off, the elevator finally opened on a crisp, contemporary lobby. Grace Davis, the receptionist, sat behind her round desk with a phone receiver tucked beneath her chin. "Mmm-hmm...mmm-hmm..." she mumbled. She shoved back a lock of wispy red hair that had fallen from the bun at her nape, and rolled her eyes at Penny from behind her small, gold-framed glasses as if to say the person on the phone wouldn't shut up.

"I'll just go on back," Penny whispered, pointing. Then she padded toward the hallway that led to the private offices, her heart rising to her throat. She was about to do this, about to deliver this crazy, demanding note to sensible, *un*demanding Martin, who would likely think she was off her rocker the moment he saw it.

Don't think like that, she commanded herself. You've got to do this. And maybe he'll even like it. Maybe it will even *unleash* the animal hidden inside him. If there *was* an animal hidden inside him. Oh please, Penny thought desperately, let there be an animal. Even if it's just a little one.

She prayed she was right because the startling fact Penny had figured out about herself over the past few days was that an animal lurked inside *her*.

Okay, so it was a slightly timid animal at this point. Yet when she'd realized she might soon commit herself to one man for the rest of her life, it had dawned on her that not only did she have sexual desires that were going unfulfilled, but they were sort of *wild* sexual desires. Dating a guy without passion...that was okay. But when she imagined getting *married*, the package came with great sex.

She'd never known that before now, but maybe she'd always just been waiting, assuming that part of her life—a true, maybe even hedonistic sexual awakening—would come along later. She'd meet some perfect man who would set all her inhibitions free and lead her through the thrilling, reckless affair of a lifetime....

But it hadn't happened yet, and if it was going to happen with Martin, she would clearly have to give him a push in the right direction. It would be worth it in the end, she promised herself as she stuck her head into his corner office to find it blessedly empty. It'll be worth it tonight when she swept him off his feet and *he* loved it and *she* loved it and a whole new sexual landscape unfurled before them both. Actually, just thinking of the plan she'd formulated this morning was enough to leave her mildly aroused. Oh yes, she thought, suddenly imbued with a sexy new nip of confidence, this was going to be good. This was going to be very good.

Her heart actually pumped with more excitement than fear as she lowered the bag onto Martin's desk in the middle of the scattered papers and folders. Her little surprise would be the perfect thing to take his mind off business, and it would be a wonderful, even generous way to send him off to his software conference in Las Vegas.

Turning the note toward the desk chair where he'd see it first thing upon sitting down, Penny pivoted and scurried from the room. Then she went about the business of distributing the rest of the sandwiches to the appointed offices, finishing with the new guy, Ryan. He didn't have a nameplate outside his door yet, but had been occupying the tiny office next to the conference room for the past week.

Heading back toward the elevator, Penny reimmersed herself in thoughts of the night to come. When she returned to the restaurant, she needed to call the limo service, then break it to Patti that she was leaving early to shop for something special to wear.

She flinched to a stop just before barreling head-on into the dark suit and bright tie that suddenly loomed before her. "Oh!" She lifted her eyes, expecting to find Martin, relieved to see that it was only Ryan, who was taller and considerably broader in the shoulders than she'd realized before. "Hi."

"Hi," he replied, although his smile looked a little off-kilter, questioning, and it didn't take a genius to figure out why; Penny probably looked as nervous as if she'd just made off with the petty cash drawer.

"I, uh, was just..." What was she thinking? Was she going to explain that she was busy preparing to ravish his boss? "Enjoy your lunch," she said instead, then skirted past him toward the elevators without sparing him another thought.

She had more important things on her mind, after all. She had a seduction to orchestrate.

AFTER GRABBING A SODA from the machine in the break-room, Ryan Pierce slid into the big leather chair in his new boss's corner office, ready to get back to work. He wasn't sorry Martin had left town a day earlier than planned; it meant a quiet first Friday on the job, and it gave Ryan a lot more space to spread out, not to mention a much better view.

Martin had suggested Ryan study some of the pre-miere software applications the company had created over the past few years, the ones they used to showcase their wares to potential clients. Only Ryan's computer hadn't arrived from Martin's wholesale supplier yet, leaving Ryan to work from his own personal laptop, so Martin had offered up *his* computer for viewing the programs while he was away. He'd also asked Ryan to keep a check on his e-mail; if anything came in that sounded urgent, Ryan could make sure someone dealt with it.

Forcing his gaze from the bright, sunny downtown streets, he spun the chair toward the desk where Penny the Sandwich Girl, as he thought of her, had left his lunch. Reaching toward the brown bag that bore the same Two Sisters logo on it as the baseball cap she always wore, he noticed something extra today—a company card stapled to the top of the bag.

His mouth fell open as he read it.

She wanted him to meet her? Tonight? And she wanted him to be ready for *anything*?

He was a sharp guy and it generally took a lot to baffle him, but at this, he literally reached up to scratch his head. Then he read the note again. And ripped into the bag.

Unwrapping the sandwich, he flipped through it as one might a stack of papers to confirm that *he* had the right sandwich and *she* had the right guy. Sure enough, ham and Swiss on rye with mayo. This was too weird.

After a moment's contemplation, however, Ryan could only conclude that this was her slightly offbeat way of asking him on a date. It was an unusual approach, to say the least, but maybe she was just too nervous to ask in person. Come to think of it, she'd *seemed* pretty nervous when he'd passed her in the hallway a few minutes ago, and now he knew why. She'd just dropped an invitation sandwich on his desk. He'd also noticed she was sort of chummy with Grace, who must've told Penny he was working in Martin's office today.

Leaning back in the large chair, Ryan couldn't help feeling just a little arrogant. Less than a week in a new city and a cute girl had already asked him out. And she *was* cute. He'd noticed the delicate face and big blue eyes underneath that baseball cap, not to mention the pretty swath of long sandy-blond hair cascading through the hat's back opening. She generally wore a loose T-shirt and shorts, so he hadn't exactly gotten a look at her shape, but he knew she had nice legs. Appearance aside, she was friendly, too, always ready with an easy smile, and he'd heard her giggling good-naturedly with Grace more than once as they'd stood chatting in the lobby.

Granted, he and Penny had never actually shared a one-on-one conversation other than the awkward enjoy-your-lunch exchange just a minute ago, but suddenly that "enjoy your lunch" had taken on new meaning. Maybe her friendly smiles were more than friendly. Maybe her easy hellos were attempts at flirtation, only he'd had his head buried too deeply in his new job to notice.

And if any other girl had tossed a line like, "Be ready for anything" at him, Ryan might've backed off. He'd just moved here from Chicago to get a new start, and part of that meant settling down, walking the straight and narrow, and avoiding *anything* that might get him into trouble. But Penny the Sandwich Girl seemed... harmless. Too cute to be wild. And the way Ryan saw it, that made her the perfect girl for him. New city, new job, and now a nice, down-to-earth girl to date.

So sure he'd meet her tonight. Ten o'clock. Corner of Fourth and Walnut. While he might not be ready for anything, he would go prepared for a nice, fun, uncomplicated evening with a nice, fun, uncomplicated girl.

As THE LUNCH RUSH WANED and the restaurant began to empty, Penny called Patti over to the long, mahogany bar where she was removing half-filled glasses and dirty plates to a tub bound for the dishwasher.

"Whatcha need?" Patti approached the bar clutching a damp rag in her fist.

Penny widened her eyes as if to say *pleeeeease*. "An afternoon off. *This* afternoon, in fact. Do you mind if I leave after we get the lunch mess under control?"

Patti tilted her head in response, her long, light-brown hair falling over one shoulder. "What for?"

"Well, you know Martin's going out of town tomorrow, right? So I want to plan a...special evening with him before he goes. Before I make my decision."

Patti's mouth dropped open. "Pen, you can't seriously be thinking of marrying him. I mean, are you? Really?"

Penny pursed her lips in irritation. "Yes, I am. Really." Most of the time, Penny accepted her older sister's well-meaning wisdom, but at the moment, she felt uncharacteristically bold. "What of it?"

Patti blinked. "Touchy."

"Well, you would be, too, if I said something like that to you."

"I'm sorry," Patti said. "But I'm worried about this decision of yours. You haven't known the guy long enough to be marrying him."

"I've known him for two years!"

"He's been a *customer* for two years. That's not the same as knowing him."

"Even so, we get along great, we like the same things, we respect each other's ambitions, and he's a really nice person. So what if I haven't been dating him forever? If something works, it works. Right?"

Patti narrowed her gaze on Penny. "Don't take this the wrong way," she said softly, "but don't you think Martin is just a little...boring?"

Penny sighed, for more reasons than she could easily name. When it came right down to it, wasn't she really pretty boring herself? Oh, she was fairly witty on her good days and she got along well with people, but it wasn't as if she was the life of every party. In fact, Patti's accusation seemed as good an argument as any in *favor* of marrying Martin.

And she also guessed it hurt a little to have her sister cast aspersions on a man she liked and cared for. She felt the need to defend him, both for his sake and hers. "Maybe he's *not* so boring."

"Oh?" Patti lifted her eyebrows.

"Ask me tomorrow," Penny said with a coy grin.

"Ah." Patti nodded knowingly. "You haven't slept with him yet."

Penny chose not to answer, but suspected the warmth climbing her cheeks replied for her.

"Well then, by all means, take the rest of the day off. There are enough servers on the clock to keep things under control, and if the guy's leaving tomorrow, I certainly don't want to prevent the big event from taking place."

"Thanks," Penny said quietly, although she couldn't help feeling the unspoken part of Patti's words, as well—*I don't want to prevent you from finding out he's boring in bed, too.*

On every other level—family, friends, the successful business they'd built together—she and Patti always saw eye to eye and treated each other like equals. But when it came to guys, romance, love, Penny always felt as if she were behind in the game, as if Patti knew more than her. She didn't understand why, since they'd both had their fair share of serious relationships, and they both remained relatively confident, content, single women. But maybe Patti had always been just a little more adventurous, a little more knowledgeable about sex, a little more...everything.

Well, Penny hoped her sister was wrong about Martin. She hoped by the time the sun rose tomorrow morning, she'd be able to announce that he was indeed *not* boring, and that they were fabulously, wildly compatible in bed. *Take that, Patti.*

And it really would happen, too; she could just feel it. Everything was going to go her way. After all, Patti would probably drop over in a dead faint if she knew some of the stuff—the fantasies—that had played through Penny's mind lately. She hardly knew where they were coming from, but if someone as straitlaced as Penny had a secret side, then surely Martin did, too. Now, to find it.

As Penny made the phone call to secure a limousine, then grabbed up her purse to set out shopping, she put more of tonight's plan in place in her head. She'd figured if she was going to go through with this seduction business, she might as well go all the way. So she'd sifted through her growing sexual desires and picked out an easily realized fantasy, one of several that'd always been a loosely formed thought, yet which had gathered into something more solid in her mind over the past days.

Stepping out into the hot summer sun that beat down on the city sidewalk, she glanced at the large digital clock jutting from the corner of the building. It was almost two. T minus eight hours and her fantasy would begin, and Martin would get the thrill of his life.

SEVEN AND A HALF HOURS LATER, Penny sat behind the black limousine's tinted windows, feeling like someone else. Which stood to reason, since she'd paused before the mirror in her foyer not long ago trying to figure out who she saw there. With hair volumized by electric rollers that hadn't seen the light of day since high school, makeup that somehow changed the entire appearance of her face, and especially with the little black dress and strappy heels she wore, it was no wonder she couldn't recognize herself.

She'd instructed the driver to stop the limo at the corner of Fourth and Walnut at precisely ten o'clock where a gentleman would be joining her. Only now, as she rode in unnerving silence, did she begin to wonder if the stoic thirty-something driver suspected what was about to happen back here. She pressed the button that raised a dark panel between them.

Eyeing the bottle of champagne in the ice bucket, Penny reached for it. She'd intended to save it for Martin and his seduction, but she needed it now. Hopefully it would calm her down. Filling one of the long, fluted glasses provided, she drained it by half, then paused as the bubbly, tingling sensation skittered through her.

Drinking another quick glass and a half as they neared downtown, she thought she was almost relaxed. But then, maybe *relaxed* was the wrong word. As it had earlier in Martin's office, fear was beginning to give way to anticipation.

Her fantasy was to make wild love to a man in a moving limousine. It was fairly simple as fantasies went, she supposed, but that made it attainable, too, and something about it just sounded so glamorous and urgent. Although she'd never experienced it, she'd always been fascinated by the idea of two people so truly impassioned that they couldn't even wait to get home.

The limo tooled around the downtown streets, moving past Fountain Square, turning right onto Walnut, soon passing the awning-covered entrance to the Two Sisters Pub, still open for business on a Friday night. But Penny's thoughts had nothing to do with work. Instead, she pondered the black push-up bra and thong panties beneath her dress. No one who knew her would believe she even owned such things, let alone wore them. Oh, she'd always liked pretty lingerie, but the stuff she had on tonight, underneath *and* on top, fell into a different category. Even she could scarcely believe that good girl Penny Halloran could be this utterly wild! She bit her lip and silently thanked God for inventing champagne.

Yet as she gazed out the tinted windows as they circled the block, she suffered a startling thought. What if somehow the windows weren't really tinted well enough? What if somehow people on the street or in other cars could actually see in? She knew it was a crazy thought, but the idea of being seen was almost enough to squelch the delicious bit of naughtiness that had begun to bite pleasantly into her spine. She wanted to be wild, she wanted to give herself over to complete abandon, she wanted to be *everything* for the man she was about to seduce, but she also wanted to shut out the rest of the world, make sure they both knew they were the only two people involved.

So Penny reached up and drew the tiny shade over the window next to her, snapping it shut at the bottom, then moved about the whole interior of the limo, darkening every window the same way.

When she was done, the inside of the car was as black as a cave. Martin wouldn't be able to see her—her voluminous hair, her crimson lips, her sexy, clinging dress. But at least he would be able to *feel* that part, then peel it off her, so maybe that was all that mattered. Their hands, their bodies—all exploring and connecting. And of course, if she really *did* want Martin to see her, she could easily flip on the overhead light.... But maybe, she decided, this whole thing would be easier to accomplish in the dark.

With that in mind, Penny reached up to the car's ceiling and located the switch that controlled the interior light. Shifting it until the overhead bulb came on, she studied the settings: On, Off and Door. She didn't even want Martin to see her when he stepped inside the car, so she moved the switch to Off, immersing herself in a darkness that wouldn't be interrupted when the door opened.

The truth was, an old nemesis had begun to return over the last few minutes. Fear, nervousness. She'd never done anything so completely contrary to her normal self, and at the moment—champagne or no champagne—she was beginning to grow uncertain if she could pull this off without feeling like an idiot. What on earth would Martin think? What if he didn't like it? What if he thought she was easy, sleazy? What had she been thinking to rent a limousine just for the purpose of having sex in it?

Penny was a heartbeat away from forgetting the whole idea of seduction, and instead trying to convince Martin she'd intended nothing more than a fun evening of champagne and barhopping on Main Street, when the limo pulled to the curb, gliding to a slow stop.

They were at Fourth and Walnut; Penny could feel it.

And somehow, just arriving there, just knowing she stood on the very brink of either embracing her desires or running from them, girded her strength in a way she'd never imagined.

Penny swallowed hard, determined to take this bold leap into sexual abandon without looking back. This was it, the beginning of something wild.

AS RYAN PUSHED THROUGH the revolving brass doors that led out to Walnut Street, the sultry summer air hit him like a brick. He thought to reach up and loosen his tie, but instead tightened it a little instead, wanting to look good for his date, or at least as good as a guy could look after working fourteen hours straight. It had seemed silly to drive home, then come back to meet Penny, when there was plenty he could do at the office. He intended to make a good impression on Martin and go places in this company, and he figured there was no time to start like the present.

The glow of streetlamps lit the city night, but when he glanced at the corner she'd indicated on her note, no one was there.

Well, no one but whoever sat in that shiny black limo. A matching black-clad driver stood at the car's door.

Ryan shifted his gaze to the green awning bearing the familiar Two Sisters logo—a cartoonish line drawing of two women, one holding up a hamburger, the other a mug of beer—and wondered if Penny might be inside. But no, she'd said the corner, so he'd wait there for a few minutes before looking elsewhere.

When he checked his watch at five after ten, he glanced up to see that the limo still lingered. And only then did it dawn on him. Could *she* possibly be inside it?

Nah, surely not. Not Penny the Sandwich Girl.

Yet for some reason he kept staring at the limo, and the longer he stared, the more he began to think, maybe. After all, the damn thing had been sitting at the corner since he'd walked out at ten on the dot. It seemed an elaborate first date, but the idea that she was inside began to press on him.

Even as he took a few tentative steps toward the big,

black car, he actually debated forgetting this whole thing. He had the odd sense now that perhaps this "uncomplicated girl" was a little more complicated than she'd seemed. Yet something, call it curiosity, a simple Alice-in-Wonderland need to see what lay down the rabbit hole, drew him toward the car.

His heartbeat increased as he got nearer, wondering what awaited him. And even as his better judgment told him to turn around and walk away, to go get a drink somewhere by himself and then go home, curiosity bloomed into a pinch of excitement in his chest.

"I'm supposed to meet a woman here named Penny," he said to the driver.

The man responded by opening the car's door.

Ryan stepped into the cool air of the limousine with total confidence. Only when he sat down and the door shut behind him did he realize he'd been immersed in total darkness.

"Are you surprised?"

Ryan tried to formulate an answer, at least relieved to hear that the voice *did* belong to Penny.

"Wait, don't answer that," she said as the limo pulled away from the curb. "In fact, don't say anything at all. Let me do all the talking. I'm sure you find this pretty unconventional, but I just had to do it. I just wanted to do...something special, something crazy, something wild. For once in my life, I just wanted to lose all my inhibitions, so..." she paused to swallow audibly, nervously "...I hope you won't think this is awful of me. I hope it's a part of me you'll be able to...fully appreciate, since, in all honesty, it's a side of myself I just discovered and I want to get—" her voice dropped to a provocative tone now "—*really* intimate. So just sit back, relax, and let me make you feel good."

As she'd spoken, Ryan had kept waiting for his eyes to adjust to the darkness, but it wasn't happening. Still, he'd sensed her drawing nearer across the dark confines of the limo until she knelt next to him in the seat. Her knees nudged his hip and her breath warmed his neck just before she lowered a soft, sexy kiss there.

He'd been trying to remain very still, very quiet, but lost both wars when her hand slid up his thigh. He leaned his head back with a tiny groan that came all the way from his gut. But he still didn't say anything, either too startled by the whole situation or simply obeying her orders, he didn't know. And he wasn't exactly giving it close examination; he remained much busier trying to survive the shock, and immediate pleasure, that had assaulted him upon climbing into the car.

Penny drew in her breath as she pressed her palm into the crotch of his pants, making him gasp, and— Oh, he was already getting hard. She bit her lip, relieved and amazed that this was working. That quickly, it was a success she could feel between them, a mutual need escalating at an incredible speed.

He'd stayed blissfully quiet upon her request and it'd somehow made it much easier to move close to him, begin touching him. She'd felt his quick response in the arch of his neck against her lips and, of course, in her hand. Drawn totally into the seduction, she rose and lifted one stocking-clad knee across his lap to straddle him, the heat of his body fusing instantly with hers.

When his palms molded to her thighs, then slid smoothly up to the hem of her dress, Penny took another deep breath and did what suddenly came all too naturally. Covering his hands with hers, she guided them higher, *under* the dress.

His fingers edged past the tops of her stockings,

crossing bare skin before coming to rest on her hips, and he released another small moan. She didn't know whether it was because she had so boldly invited the touch or because he'd discovered how little she wore beneath her dress; she only knew she liked it.

She ran her fingertips through his thick hair and leaned near his ear. "Are you as turned on as I am? I want to be really sexy for you." Her voice came out shaky, not from nervousness now, but from excitement.

"Uh..."

She giggled, then moved a teasing finger to his lips. "No, shh, don't answer. Just kiss me."

Twining her arms about his neck, Penny leaned in for a no-holds-barred kiss like she'd never given Martin before. Electricity spiraled through her as he returned it, fully, passionately, with an underlying power she wouldn't have believed Martin could possess. She had the sensation of him somehow holding back even as he gave her everything she wanted, needed, and she feared that if he really let go of his desire, it might actually overwhelm her.

He deepened the kiss further, pushing his tongue into her mouth, and she moaned at the hot, tender invasion. His hands drifted to her bottom, which was bare but for the thin strip of fabric running up the center, to press her more snugly against the incredible hardness in his pants. Penny had never felt anything like the fire now intensifying between them. Even as the darkened encounter stayed steamy, slow, hot, it also grew more urgent. Urgency was not just part of the fantasy any longer; it was a pulsing reality.

She wanted to go slow, keep the steamy and hot in place, make this aching pleasure last as long as possible.

Yet at the same time, she wanted to go further. She wanted to undress him.

She worked at his tie and he leaned his head back to give her better access. Then she unbuttoned his shirt, pushing it open. She ran her hands down his bare chest, exploring the broad muscles and firm planes she'd never envisioned Martin concealing beneath his business suit.

As the limo came to a slow stop, he pulled his hands from under the dress, reaching around until she heard the zipper at her back being lowered. Grazing his fingertips across her shoulders with a feather-soft touch, he drew the bodice to her waist, and even in the dark, she felt beautiful and wild and freer than ever in her life.

His hands rose to her breasts, caressing, kneading through the lace that still covered them, his thumbs stroking across the firm, beaded peaks. By the time the limo accelerated again, she was panting and grinding, rubbing his chest.

He fumbled at the front of her bra.

"In the back," she breathed.

But he didn't even bother reaching behind her this time, his breath having grown as labored as hers. He found the thin straps on her shoulders and yanked them down, his hands sliding into the lace cups to take sweet possession of her breasts. "Oh yes," she murmured at the startling sensation of his touch against her bare, aching flesh. "Yes. Yes!"

But no, no, she had to calm down. Because she wanted to stretch out the pleasure as long as she could. She could scarcely believe she was doing this, feeling these things, yet that remained secondary to the knowledge that she wanted more of this marvelous touching, and she knew he wanted it, too.

"Do you want me to get out of this dress for you?"

He only groaned. His way of saying *please*. She felt it.

Crossing her arms to grab hold of the fabric that had pooled at her waist, Penny removed the dress over her head in one brisk movement and flung it behind her. Then, running her hands over his broad shoulders, she kissed him deeply, more heat swirling between her thighs with each feverish connection of their mouths. He caressed her breasts, lightly pinching her nipples between surprisingly skilled fingertips until Penny thought she'd lose her mind.

Only when his hands lowered to wind around the thin elastic at her hips, however, did she understand that it was time for more. And she was ready now. *Very* ready.

She rose up on her knees before him.

Savored the sensation of having her panties lowered over her thighs, past the lace edges of her stockings.

Heard her own ragged breath as she pressed her palms against the roof for balance when the limo turned a corner. Heard the whimpers leave her throat as he held her hips, then stroked both his thumbs up the center of her, one after the other, playing her like an instrument.

But just as quickly as the hot touches melted her, his hands moved down to her panties again. "Take them off." It was the barest of whispers, the only words he'd spoken, all powerful in their brevity.

Penny backed away quickly to the seat across from him and shimmied out of the undies, her anticipation rising. And then something released inside her like steam from a radiator when the cap comes off, a burning need that couldn't be denied a minute longer. She didn't care about going slow anymore, she just wanted the man, now.

Climbing back onto his lap, she reached for his belt buckle.

He drew her close, drew her breast into his hungry mouth, forcing her to cry out and making it considerably harder to get his pants undone. But Penny worked vigorously anyway, her hands trapped between them, and only when she reached into the opening of his underwear did he loosen his grip, letting her lean back on him.

Holding him in her hand, trying not to faint with the wonder of it, her voice came out raspy. "I wanted to do this all night, make it last. But I can't wait anymore."

She lowered her body onto his and they both moaned at the blunt, intimate connection. Even in the dark, even with this man whom she'd never truly felt that close to before, Penny knew a union, a soul-binding bliss, she'd never experienced or even thought possible. "I...I didn't know...sex could be like this," she whispered.

His hand found the back of her head then, bringing her down for another of his heart-stopping kisses. Penny sank into it, into the intense and mounting pleasure as she moved on him, his body pumping rhythmically up into hers. She raked her sensitive nipples against his chest, clutched at his neck, and felt the tumultuous waves gathering inside her...until they crashed over her in sweet, shattering release.

Thrashing against him, riding it out, she leaned her head back and basked in the deepest physical fulfillment she'd ever known. Yet just as her climax began to wane, he groaned beneath her and pushed her hips down as he thrust upward, again and again, soon growling his own pleasure in her ear. And wondrously, his climax, coming so close on the heels of hers, somehow added an extra tiny burst of sensation deep in her core, seeming to stretch her orgasm out a little longer, just when she'd thought it was over.

"Ohh," Penny sighed, still caught up in the mind-blowing sensations and trying to come back down to earth. But whether she was up or down, she knew one thing for sure—the experience she'd just shared with this man had moved her so deeply, twisted her heart, soul and body so profoundly, that it had erased all doubt. It had erased everything but the perfection that was them—together.

"Oh yes!" she cried out. "Yes! I'll marry you!"

Yet at her proclamation, the body beneath her went instantly, dreadfully still. "Wait just a minute here. Who said anything about marriage?"

Penny turned cold as her heart sank like a stone. The voice she'd just heard didn't belong to Martin.

2

PENNY REACHED OVERHEAD and flipped on the light inside the limo...then screamed and flung herself to the opposite seat. Oh God, it was the guy from Martin's office, Ryan! And they'd just...they'd just...!

Using one hand to yank her bra up and the other to snatch her dress from the floor and press it over her nakedness, she gaped at him, realizing he looked almost as shocked as she felt. "What did you...?" she began. "I mean, how did you...? I mean, where's *Martin?*"

He leaned forward, his eyes wide, his mouth dropping open in disbelief. *"Where's Martin?* Somewhere in Flagstaff, I guess. What the hell does that have to do with anything?"

Martin was in Flagstaff? Arizona? What in the world was he doing in Flagstaff? And in the meantime, Ryan just sat there doing nothing to cover himself, his shirt hanging open, his broad chest looking just as good as it had felt under her fingertips, and the sight of him wasn't helping things at all. "I thought you were him, of course," she snapped.

"Of course?" He sounded incredulous, and only then did it hit her.

"Oh, you're new in town. Maybe you don't know..." She swallowed. "I—we—Martin and I are..." Oh, what on earth were they? "A couple," she finally concluded.

He gave a slight this-explains-it-all nod, saying,

"Ah," simply, sharply, although Penny thought plenty still needed to be explained.

Nonetheless, she could barely let herself focus on the guy, because even unkempt and rumpled, he looked... well, way better than she'd ever noticed up in Martin's office. And also because she was naked and they'd just...they'd just...

Her eyes darted about the limo, to the ceiling, the floor, her own nudity... *Dear God, how can I get this dress on if he's just going to keep sitting there staring at me?*

Finally meeting his gaze head-on and trying to forget her lack of clothing, Penny felt the overpowering urge to come completely clean with him. "Look, it's like this," she blurted, speaking quickly. "Martin asked me to marry him, but we'd never, um, had sex. So I decided to just—just do something *wild* with him, something to try to bring out the animal in him. I thought it would be fun and adventurous to live out a fantasy, and I— Oh God, I can't believe this just happened!"

By the time she finished, he was holding up his hands, as if asking for mercy. "Listen, you don't need to tell me all this. It's all right. You don't need to...to..."

His words made her realize what she'd done—she'd just told this guy things about herself she'd never told another human being. "But I *do* need to," she insisted. "I need you to know this isn't what I intended. I mean, it is, but I was planning on it with a different guy, a guy that I...uh...*knew,* for heaven's sake. And I need you to know that I'm not, not...really what you, uh..." she glanced down at her bareness once more "...see here before you. I'm really that girl who delivers sandwiches and wears...clothing. Usually *loose* clothing. This girl, this girl is...someone I just made up, just for tonight, and she isn't real and she isn't me, and—" A tremendous sadness washed over her, a desperation to redeem herself in his eyes. "Please don't think what you must be thinking of me! Please just forget this ever happened!"

Even as stunned as Ryan remained, at the moment it all took a back seat to the compassion he felt for her, with her eyes so glassy, her voice so frantic. He hated the panic glimmering in her pretty gaze.

There were a million things he wanted to tell her. How sexy she was, how beautiful. That he didn't think less of her for what had just happened, but that she *must* be the woman she claimed she'd made up, because you couldn't fake that. And despite his shock and helplessness, there was no way in hell he'd ever be able to forget such outstanding sex. Instead, though, he just stayed quiet, as he had through the other, better part of their encounter, because he had a feeling she wouldn't believe or even want to hear any of the thoughts playing through his head.

"Martin is in...Flagstaff?" she finally asked.

Ryan nodded. "He left a day early. A last-minute decision to see a client out there."

"But how did you...?" Her voice trailed off as her head tilted in confusion.

"I got a note on my sandwich from you."

"*Martin's* sandwich."

"No, I checked, it was mine. Ham and swiss on—"

"Rye with mayo," she finished for him.

He nodded, this other piece of the picture slowly becoming clear.

"Same sandwich," she murmured.

"How about that," he replied lamely.

Penny gave her head a slight shake. "I didn't know. My sister made some of the sandwiches today."

But Ryan was way past the sandwiches already, and feeling sheepish. "When I saw the note, I thought you were asking me out."

Across from him, she nodded, still sitting there in a bra and stockings, her dress tossed over her. His gaze kept dropping to her bare hip, to the curves so visible behind what the dress covered. He really did think she was beautiful and sexy, and despite himself, he could feel hints of arousal rising again already.

"I'm sorry," he said then, although he wasn't entirely sure what for. Still thinking about her body even after her heart-wrenching pleas? Or simply being arrogant enough to think she would ask him out without even knowing him, arrogant enough to approach a limousine, thinking it was there for him?

Well, she'd been right about one thing—he should've been ready for anything, should've heeded that warning. A nervous quiet lingered between them and he wished he could take his eyes off her, but with a nearly naked woman sitting across from him...well, where else was he gonna look?

"I'm the one who's sorry," she finally said. "I mean, even in the dark, you'd think I'd recognize..."

He nodded, agreeing.

"But then, I just now noticed—" she gave him a timid once-over "—you look like him, kind of."

He nodded again. It was true. He and Martin were about the same height, shared the same basic build, and wore their medium-brown hair in a similar style. "Yeah, kind of." Then he forced a laugh, despite the fact that nothing was very funny.

"I'm trying to let that make me feel better," she said, "like it's a mistake anyone could've made, but..." Her eyes dropped shut and she lifted her hands to cover her mouth, as if she were replaying the moment in her mind all over again.

Ryan's heart tightened into a tense knot and he felt the inclination to reach out and touch her knee to comfort her, but that would be the wrong move. "Listen, don't feel bad," he said instead. "I...don't think badly of you, honest."

She raised her gaze. "But I just..." She closed her eyes once more as if to shut out what had happened, then opened them wide. "Oh God, I just seduced you! I had my way with you! I didn't even give you a choice!"

Ryan swallowed, then spoke quietly. "I had a choice."

They peered at each other in uncomfortable silence until she said, "Would you mind if I turned the light back out so I can get dressed?"

"Sure."

"And maybe you could, uh—" she motioned vaguely toward him "—fix *your* clothes, too."

At this, he flinched. He'd been too caught up in what was happening to realize he still sat there unbuttoned and undone. "Um, yeah, sure thing. Sorry about that."

The return of darkness was more jarring than Ryan anticipated. For a few brief seconds, he wondered what she would do if he reached out to find her in the blackness and began to kiss her again, touch her, make love to her again. He wondered if it wouldn't be simpler to just go back a few minutes in time, back to her thinking he was someone else and back to him thinking she wanted him, if it wouldn't be easier to just leave the lights off and pretend. But they were only fleeting thoughts that made no sense, so Ryan tucked and buttoned until everything was back in place save for the tie hanging loose about his neck.

When the rustling of fabric and sounds of sliding zippers ceased, and the overhead light illuminated the car once more, Penny pointed to a bottle of champagne jutting from an ice bucket. "Want some?"

Lifting the open bottle from the ice, Ryan noticed it was half-empty. "Looks like you got started without me."

"I needed it for courage," she admitted. "Now I just need to be drunk." Taking the bottle from his hand, she tipped it to her mouth and took a hefty swig.

"Sounds like a decent idea," he said. She passed the bottle back and he swallowed a long drink, too, then spoke uncertainly. "I guess I should, uh, tell the driver to take me to the parking garage."

Her slight hesitation made him wonder if maybe she didn't want him to go, if maybe she actually wanted to drink and commiserate together, but it was not to be. "Um, yeah," she said with a definite degree of finality.

Looking over his shoulder, Ryan opened the privacy panel and gave the driver directions to where he parked his car. He grew suddenly embarrassed on Penny's behalf, wondering if the guy had heard anything.

Thankfully, though, the driver's eyes betrayed nothing, and Ryan shut the panel, leaving him and Penny awkwardly alone again. As the limo continued winding through the downtown streets, they stayed quiet, simply passing the champagne back and forth until he offered her the bottle one final time with the words, "Last drink?" She took it, emptied it, then chucked it back in the ice bucket.

She looked so despondent. Ryan wanted to hug her, tell her again it was all right, but this time do it while peering into her eyes and maybe stroking her hair.

But she was practically *engaged* to his boss, for God's sake—or at least that's what he thought she'd said—and things were horrible enough already without him doing something stupid, such as being tender with her.

As the long black car finally glided across the echoing garage toward the only vehicle still there, Ryan leaned forward and met her gaze. Despite this being what she wanted, and despite the fact that she belonged to his brand-new boss, he felt bad leaving her after what they'd done together. "Are you gonna be all right?" he asked, and this time he *did* touch her knee.

She started to tremble—he felt it beneath his fingertips—and, taking a deep breath, she lifted her gaze. "Yeah. I guess."

But when he reached for the door handle and began to step out of the car, she grabbed his wrist. He glanced back to find her eyes looking frantic again. "You won't tell Martin about this?"

Tell his boss he'd just had wild sex with his girlfriend? "No, definitely not. It'll stay just between us. Promise."

"Thank you."

Not bothering to point out that she wasn't the only one with something to lose, he exited the limo, took one last look at her sitting there wearing her sexy dress and a distressed expression, then closed the door.

RYAN SAT DOWN behind Martin's desk early the next morning, although even sitting in the man's chair felt intrusive now, as if he were trespassing. He vowed not to think about that, though, since he'd come here to work. The office lay desolate on a Saturday morning, but it was just as well; it would help him concentrate, stay focused. All this work would get him firmly entrenched in Schuster Systems' operations, and it also seemed his only hope of getting his mind off what had happened last night, since hours of tossing and turning in bed hadn't done it.

He shook his head as the unsettling truth assaulted him once more. Already this felt like another disaster in the making, another fist with a choke hold on his career. Unfortunately, this wasn't the first mistake Ryan had ever made.

Only two months ago, he'd lost his job at ComData in Chicago, for missing a client meeting of all things. A missed meeting was an embarrassing *faux pas*, definitely, but he hadn't believed it would earn him a pink slip until it had happened.

It had all occurred innocently enough. He'd planned to have dinner with a woman he'd recently met, then hook up afterward with David Collins and Roger Borcherding, the top guys at Fischer International, in their hotel lounge for drinks around nine. Ryan had been assigned to manage their system conversion and the two executives had suggested touching base that evening after their flight arrived.

Ryan had picked up his date, Maggie, at her office after work, planning to eat and return her to her car by eight-thirty, but he'd been having so much fun that the first time he'd looked at his watch, it was quarter to nine.

Then, after hurriedly paying the bill and racing back to Maggie's car, they discovered it had a flat tire.

Maggie encouraged him to go ahead, but Ryan refused to leave her there alone in the dark, waiting for help to come. After assuring her that staying wouldn't be a problem, he called the hotel and asked to have a message delivered to the two men waiting in the bar.

Then he changed the tire, and followed Maggie home to make sure she was okay.

When he finally reached the hotel around ten-thirty, however, he discovered that not only had his message never made it to the lounge, but Collins and Borcherding were angry. He knew he'd cut it too close on time in the first place, but he'd been sure they'd understand the position he'd been in with Maggie's car, sure that any decent guy would've handled it the same way.

All they could see, however, was that he'd stood them up, wasted their time, and proven himself irresponsible. It had made such a bad impression that Fischer International had ultimately dropped ComData and gone elsewhere for its software needs, and in the process pretty much made Ryan out to be the devil incarnate.

He still remembered standing in Mr. Lever's office, numb, trying to absorb the unbelievable results of that night. "We can't afford these kinds of screwups, Ryan," Lever had said. "And we can't afford to have someone on our team who doesn't put us first. It's nothing personal, but we have to let you go."

Ryan propped his elbows on the desk in Martin's office, then began to rub his temples as he recalled the incident.

The job loss had been devastating financially—he'd had a mortgage on a high-rise condo overlooking Lake Michigan, and he sent money home to his elderly parents in rural Indiana every month, money they needed to make ends meet.

And the job loss had also devastated him personally. He recalled standing there thinking, *This isn't the kind of guy I am, the kind of guy who gets fired from jobs; this isn't how things are supposed to be.* And it had happened all because he'd been having too much fun flirting with a woman to keep an eye on the clock. He didn't think he'd ever made such a bonehead move.

But then, the truth was, even before the fiasco at ComData, his social life had gotten him into trouble. He'd been the best and the brightest young system designer on his team at Futureware, also in Chicago, yet he'd also been fresh out of college and frat life. He'd lasted five years there, but too many late nights had led to too many late mornings. He'd always been the guy who came straggling into meetings long after they'd started, his tie crooked, his eyes bloodshot. He'd been young and stupid and careless.

That job he'd eventually chosen to leave on his own, but only after he'd been passed over for promotions numerous times. The fault was his, but he'd decided he just needed a new start. And things had been going great at ComData until that one tragic night. The job loss had been made even worse when Mr. Lever told Ryan he couldn't in good conscience give him any recommendations, which made it feel pretty damn personal, no matter what the guy said. And in fact, when Ryan had started applying for other system design jobs, he'd discovered that news of his blunder at ComData had already made the rounds in the Windy City, and no one wanted to hire a guy who lost big accounts. He'd effectively been blackballed in Chicago.

So...that left him with Cincinnati. Another new start. A smaller, more conservative city where he'd been sure he could buckle down, act responsibly, and finally reap the rewards of being damn good at his chosen profession. A fresh, young company with a solid track record. A nice condo with a river view. *And a scantily clad girl in a dark limo who'd turned out to be his new boss's fiancée.*

Ryan buried his head in his hands a little deeper, then thrust himself up out of the chair. Coffee. He needed coffee.

After making his way to the coffee machine, then digging in the pocket of his blue jeans for change, he reflected on the unbelievable events of the previous evening as the hot liquid trickled into the white cup below. He'd been terribly sorry to find out Penny belonged to Martin, and the more Ryan thought about it, the more it grated on him. Because the guy was his boss, and he would surely lose *this* job, too, if she started feeling guilty enough to tell. And also because he couldn't deny loving what had happened between them once he pushed all the weirdness aside.

He'd never been that swept away—dare he even think dominated—by a woman before. Not that she was rough, by any means—more sweet and sexy than rough—but she'd left him feeling thoroughly seduced, thoroughly...*taken*. He could still hear the tantalizing shift in her voice when it had edged from nervous and explanatory to seductive. He could still feel her soft curves, the lace of her barely there lingerie, the weight of her breasts in his hands. He could still feel the heat of her kiss, her moisture on his fingertips...

Flinching to discover he still stood in the bright light of the breakroom, Ryan blinked back the absorbing memories and reached for his coffee. Taking a gulp, he told himself to concentrate on work and get this woman off his mind. As much as possible anyway.

Still, as he made his way through the lobby and down the hall to Martin's office, his thoughts dwelled on her. Specifically, on how much he'd hated finding out she'd been embarrassed by that hot, sexy side of herself. He wished everything were different, that there could be more between them, that he could show her how incredibly good that part of her was.

But it's best this way. It was crazy for him to even wish for something else with her. Clearly, the girl was wilder than she even understood, or last night wouldn't have happened with *anybody*. And while there was certainly nothing wrong with being a little wild, it was not a quality he needed in a woman right now.

What he needed right now was stability, a dependable job with a dependable income and a dependable future. What he didn't need was an affair with the boss's fiancée, or girlfriend—hell, whatever she was. His mistake at ComData had thrown a wrench into his career, and getting his job at Schuster Systems had been an amazing stroke of luck, since Martin hadn't asked for references. But if Ryan lost *this* job, how would he bounce back? He had come here to start over and he couldn't afford another black mark next to his name.

He drained his coffee cup as he settled back behind the desk, needing that extra jolt of caffeine to get his mind back to work. Work, work, work. It was all that mattered here.

And hopefully last night's escapade would fade away just as she wanted it to, as they both wanted it to.

Except for the memory of the sex, of course. That wouldn't fade.

Taking a deep breath, he reached for the folder he'd plucked from his own closet-size office on his way into Martin's. Martin had dropped it in Ryan's in-box before leaving, telling him it contained the specs on his first major project at Schuster, and that he'd scheduled a planning session for Ryan with the client on Monday afternoon. It was important that this first assignment go well, so he wanted to familiarize himself with the details before the meeting two days from now.

Flipping open the folder, his gaze fell on the neatly typed job form.

Client: Two Sisters Restaurant & Pub

Contact: Penny Halloran

Oh God.

How could this be? How could fate be cruel enough to throw this woman back in his face like this?

When he finally started breathing again, his eyes dropped farther down the page to the bright yellow sticky note bearing the bold print he already recognized as Martin's.

Ryan—meet with Penny at her house on Monday, two o'clock. Grace can give you directions. M

Penny's *house?* If this wasn't awful enough already, why on earth would they meet at her *house* of all places?

Ryan swallowed, hard. This was bad. Really bad. Because unbidden images were already filling his brain.

He saw her in the black bra and panties he'd never really gotten a good look at.

He saw her atop him, in his lap, grinding.

He saw her soft, delicate hand reaching down, wrapping around him. *Oh, yes.*

And then he saw everything in this new city, everything in this new job...going horribly, irredeemably wrong...

PENNY CLOSED the payroll book, then locked the checks she'd just written in the desk. Patti had gone to the bank for change, the only server on duty was out running an errand, and Penny was glad to be alone in the quiet of the pub. Business was always slow on Saturday afternoon, Cincinnati's downtown thriving much more dur-

ing the workweek, but it was a good day to get the accounting and other behind-the-scenes work done.

She only came in on Saturdays if the workload was
heavy or if she was bored or needed a distraction from
something, and today, she definitely needed distraction. Besides, she was scheduled to spend a lot of her
time with a system designer in the coming few weeks,
so it didn't hurt to get ahead. She and Patti had decided
it was time to get the pub completely computerized
from the accounting system to the food orders.

When she'd finally dragged herself in the door last
night, Penny had found her answering machine blinking, although she'd known what she would hear even
before pressing the button. "Hi, Penny, it's Martin."
*Here we are, considering marriage, but he doesn't even expect
me to recognize his voice.* "I'm calling from Flagstaff—I
left early to meet a client. I hope you didn't try to get in
touch with me; I apologize if you were worried. I
should have called, but it was a last-minute decision,
and I've been busy since the plane touched down. I'll
call you after I reach Las Vegas, and of course, I'll look
forward to hearing your thoughts on my proposal
when I get back."

As Penny had erased the message, she'd thought it
sounded more like he'd made a business proposition
than a request to spend their lives together. But then,
Martin was Martin. A consummate businessman, and
she could respect that. And so what if he was a little…stiff?

Oh, Martin, Martin, Martin. What have I done? Despite
coming to work, it was impossible not to dwell on her
unwitting betrayal last night. She winced, recalling her
total mortification upon discovering she'd had sex with
the wrong man. And after returning home, she'd done

something she hadn't done in years—cried herself to sleep.

Sadly, she wasn't sure if the worst part was having seduced a guy she didn't even know...or having enjoyed it so darn much.

Exiting the restaurant's small office, Penny made her way behind the bar. Filling a glass with soda from the spray nozzle, she considered adding a little rum, still compelled to try drinking her mistake away. Already battling a champagne headache, however, she resisted the temptation.

Whether she liked it or not, Ryan had helped her live out a fantasy. Her breath caught as she remembered how wickedly fun and exciting it had been. Sure, she'd thought he was Martin, but no matter who he was, he'd done everything *so* right. Of course, it could be argued that she'd done most of the work, but his hands, touching her...his mouth, kissing her so thoroughly...

She'd never imagined sex with a stranger could be so good. She believed that intimacy had to be there first, before sex. Somehow, though, with him, it had seemed to happen *during* the sex. To her horror, even upon finding out he wasn't Martin, she'd still felt close to him after what they'd shared.

Setting down her glass, Penny ran her hand across the smooth, clean bar top. Another of her loosely formed fantasies involved having sex *there*. She didn't know why. Maybe it was about doing something private in an inherently public place, or maybe it had to do with sort of christening this establishment she'd built herself—along with her sister, of course. Either way, as she stood there alone with her thoughts, she found herself envisioning it easily enough, she and Ryan making passionate love on the long mahogany bar. Ryan, not Martin.

But it only made sense, she reasoned as ripples of sensation snaked down her spine. She and Ryan had shared a terrible, wonderful sort of intimacy last night. And despite her regret, this man knew how to kiss a woman, how to touch a woman. This man was... She rolled her eyes. *The wrong man to be thinking about!* She had to stop it, now. Besides, how would she ever face him again anyway?

When the pub's door opened, Penny flinched, feeling almost as if Patti could read her mind. Plunking a big leather satchel of change on the bar, Patti devilishly raised her eyebrows. "I forgot to ask earlier. *Is* he boring?"

Penny swallowed the lump that rose to her throat. "Um, no." After all, Patti had not specifically identified the "he" in question.

At this, Patti raised her eyebrows even farther. "Can I have details?"

Penny smiled. "No again."

Her sister frowned. "You're no fun."

"I don't think *he* would agree with you on that," Penny said, then wondered what she was doing, perpetuating this conversation. *I must be losing my mind.*

And she knew for certain she'd lost her mind when she looked up to see Ryan coming in the door that led from the building's lobby. This couldn't be happening, it just *couldn't!* What on earth was he doing here?

"Hi," he said. He looked incredibly sheepish. And incredibly handsome. How had she not noticed that before? Her skin tingled. "I was hoping you might be here."

"Hi," she replied, but she felt her eyebrows knitting

and her lips pursing, and knew she must look as glad to see him as she would an IRS auditor.

Wearing faded jeans and a polo shirt that revealed just a hint of the muscles she'd felt beneath her fingers last night, he stepped up to the bar, his earnest brown gaze shining on her. "Um, I was wondering if I could talk to you alone for a minute."

They both glanced at Patti, whose pale blue eyes were as round as two beer mugs. "Don't mind me," she said awkwardly. "I'll just...put this change away in the office." Hefting the satchel from the bar, she gave Penny a quick last glance, then flurried into the back.

Penny nervously returned her attention to Ryan. He'd taken a stool at the bar and was leaning forward on his elbows, bringing himself closer to her than she expected. She caught her breath, then said, "What's up?" as if they were casual friends or something.

"I just...wanted to make sure you're all right."

"Oh," she replied. *Very clever response, Penny.*

"Because last night you seemed pretty upset. I felt bad leaving you."

Oh wow, how sweet. She lifted her gaze to his and realized he'd been doing a much better job of looking her in the eye than she'd done with him so far. Still, she pulled herself together and gave what she thought was a much more convincing answer than she had last evening. "I'm really fine," she lied. "I mean, I was certainly shocked." She even faked a good-natured laugh. "But there's really nothing to do other than put it behind us."

He smiled again, a big, wide, what-a-relief smile. "Good. I'm glad you feel that way, because as it turns out, you and I are going to be working together."

Her mouth dropped open. "Pardon me?"

He added a shrug to his smile. "I just found out Martin assigned me the job of designing your computer system."

"Oh."

"So, is that all right with you?"

"Yeah. Sure." Of course it wasn't all right, but what would Martin think if she refused to work with Ryan? What possible reason could she give? "We'll just have to...put last night behind us, like I said," she added, wondering why she was still talking about it if she was so eager to put it behind them.

"Definitely." He nodded vigorously.

"Of course." She nodded right back.

"I'm really sorry. I know this will be awkward."

"It'll be fine," she insisted too desperately.

"Although I don't know why Martin wouldn't do the job himself, being...so close to you and everything."

She almost laughed then, considering that she'd physically been much closer to Ryan now than she'd ever been to Martin, but the word *close* just stirred up too many sensual memories. "Actually, Martin doesn't do much designing anymore now that the company's grown, so I knew he was assigning it to someone else."

"And I was, uh, wondering about something else, too. Martin's instructions said we were meeting at your house?"

She nodded some more. "I've been typing all my notes into my computer at home, but I've suffered a series of mishaps over the last few months."

"Mishaps?"

"Well, first, my printer broke. I bought a new one, but something's wrong with the connection, because it won't print. After that, I managed to get a diskette jammed in the floppy drive. Then last week, during a thunderstorm, lightning zapped my modem."

"Wow." He looked dumbfounded by her streak of bad luck.

"So the computer still *works*," she went on, "but I don't have any way to move the information out of it. Martin has promised to get it all fixed, but he hasn't had time yet, so he suggested that rather than wait, we just work from my place." Then it occurred to her to ask, "Is that all right? I mean, will you be okay with that?"

"Sure. Of course." He nodded.

"Okay." She felt herself nodding again, too. "Good."

"Well then," he said, pushing to his feet, "I'll, uh, look forward to getting together, talking about your needs, and trying to fulfill them." Then he cringed. "Your *system* needs, I mean."

More nodding on her part, repeatedly, almost convulsively. "Yes, right, my system needs."

"See you then," he concluded, disappearing out the door before Penny could utter another word. She finally quit nodding and simply stood there, staring after him, then reached behind her for a bottle of rum. Maybe adding just a dollop to her drink wouldn't hurt, after all.

"Wasn't that the new guy who works for Martin?"

Penny looked up, this time caught in the act of spiking her own drink, as Patti peeked cautiously from the office.

"Yeah." Penny tried to sound very casual as she wiped the bottle off with a rag—dusting, she was just dusting it, that was all—and returned it to the shelf behind the bar.

"Cute," Patti said, then gave her head a suspicious tilt. "Why did he want to talk to you alone?"

Swallowing, Penny pasted on a fake smile, something this whole bizarre situation was giving her a lot of practice with. "He's going to design our computer system. Just wanted to touch base, that's all."

"But...*alone?*" Patti raised her eyebrows.

Penny replied with a shrug. "Weird, I know, but I guess it's just because my name is listed as the main contact. Maybe he thought you were a spy or something." Then she made herself laugh, as if she'd just said something terribly humorous. "Who's on the schedule to tend bar tonight?" she asked, effectively steering Patti onto another subject, since she had no intention of discussing this one any further. Or thinking about it, either.

But that part was harder. Because if she'd started to calm down at all about last night, that was over now. Her insides had resumed doing flip-flops.

Partially because she felt sick about Martin and what she'd done and what he didn't know. And partially because she was so darned excited about seeing Ryan again.

3

ON MONDAY AFTERNOON, Penny sat on the couch in her small, tidy house, nestled on a quiet Hyde Park street, waiting for Ryan to arrive and thinking about her sister's unspoken suspicions.

"So, big meeting with that cute systems guy today, huh?" Patti had asked right in the middle of the lunch rush a couple of hours ago, customers and servers navigating the pub around them.

"Uh, yeah." Again, Penny had been the queen of casual.

Not that Patti bought it. A wicked grin had graced her face. "Is there something going on between you two that I don't know about?"

"Something going on?" Penny had repeated as if it were the most preposterous accusation she'd ever heard. "I don't even know the guy."

Now, as she waited for this guy she didn't know, but with whom something had definitely gone on, she asked herself why she hadn't just told Patti the truth. Even as mortifying as it was, and even if she often found herself at odds with her sister when they discussed their love lives, they'd always been honest with each other. Penny knew everything about Patti's sex life, from the moment she'd lost her virginity right up to the guy she'd slept with for the first time just last weekend, and Penny usually felt as equally compelled to confide in her sister.

This situation felt different, though, as if it were something so intimate she simply couldn't share it. Her silence was about more than her embarrassment over what had happened; it was about her fantasies, and for the same reason she hadn't told Patti about those either. There were just certain moments, she decided, that a woman wanted to keep all to herself, moments so intense even sisters couldn't be let in. Like her fantasies, she wanted to keep her limousine encounter with Ryan entirely private, belonging to her and no one else.

Well, it belonged to him, too, of course, but guys just didn't treasure the outstanding, individual moments of their lives the same way women did, did they? No, surely not.

And then it hit Penny—hard.

She treasured what happened! In fact, hardly a moment had passed since Friday night that their lovemaking hadn't permeated her thoughts and senses.

How the heck had that happened? How could she possibly cherish something that had taken place with a man she didn't even know? Especially when it was something that should have her quaking with guilt.

Yet again, she supposed it came back to the fantasy he'd helped her live out. Which meant it really had nothing to do with him exactly, only her and her fantasies, right?

Just then, the doorbell chimed. She nearly leapt from the couch as a familiar tingle ran the length of her body. She was about to see him again.

Smoothing back a lock of hair and wishing she'd worn something prettier, she walked to the door and took a deep breath, trying to prepare herself for the afternoon ahead. Because even if she tried to pretend otherwise, the truth was, this felt far from finished.

RYAN STOOD ON THE DOORSTEP thinking about what he'd envisioned the other day upon finding out about this meeting—her...on top of him. Ludicrous. He didn't want that and neither did she. They'd had a bizarre meeting in a limo, but they were putting it behind them now like the mature young professionals they both were.

Of course, that didn't mean a little spiral of sensation didn't bite into him when she answered the door, or that he didn't spend a fleeting thought on her black bra even when she appeared in shorts and a T-shirt. But he was a guy; sexual thoughts were supposed to be in his blood. He decided that made it okay, so long as he knew where his head and heart lay, which was in being mature and doing this job without any further intimate complications.

"Hi," he said. He found himself blinking at her uneasily. She wasn't wearing the baseball cap today and her hair fell over her shoulders in silky waves. Her dark blue eyes struck him as warm and deceivingly innocent.

"Hi." She glanced at his face, then her feet, then his face again.

They both seemed nervous already. This wasn't going to work without some radical move on his part.

"Listen," he said, stepping inside, "as I said the other day, I know this is awkward, but let's not worry about it anymore. How about this—let's just pretend this is the first time we've ever met." He held out his hand and put on a professional voice along with a professional smile. "I'm Ryan Pierce from Schuster Systems, and I'll be designing the system for your restaurant."

Her sweet smile seemed appreciative. "Penny Halloran, half owner of the Two Sisters Restaurant and Pub."

She took his hand, squeezing it gently in hers, after which they moved to the living room, to a desk where Penny had pulled up an extra chair next to her computer. Maybe this would all be okay, Ryan thought.

By the time she'd offered him a drink and returned with two glasses of iced tea, Ryan had drawn his laptop from its leather case and set it up beside Penny's monitor. "Let's get started," he suggested.

"I've made a lot of lists and typed up some questions and ideas," Penny said, sitting down next to him. She motioned to her computer screen. "Now I just hope they make some sort of sense."

Ryan smiled, but it came more naturally this time. "I'm sure we can make sense of them together and transform them into a workable system for you."

To his relief, things soon settled into a nice, easy rhythm, and before long, he felt so comfortable talking business with her that it almost shocked him. Maybe he'd not really believed things could go well, but they were. Penny filled him in on all the things she wanted the system to handle, from payroll and budget to food and drink orders, and Ryan couldn't help but be impressed by how well thought out her ideas were.

"This is great," he said. "You've done half my work for me. Now let's see if we can start putting your ideas together with mine." He turned to his laptop and pulled up the first of several screens he'd already started creating from templates at the office.

"Oh, you used our logo!"

"Yeah," Ryan replied, following her eyes to the monitor. He'd thought the system might feel more as though it belonged to her and her sister if he headed each screen with a small graphic of the Two Sisters logo. On the opening screen, the graphic appeared much larger. "I just scanned it from the card on..." Damn, he hadn't meant to bring that up again. "...my, uh, sandwich bag the other day."

She tensed at his words, but he could see she was a trouper, trying to maintain her composure. "That's great. I love it." She even met his gaze for good measure. Unfortunately, after having reminded them both of their encounter in the limo, he couldn't help looking into her eyes more deeply than seemed prudent.

She jerked her gaze back to the computer.

Good idea, he thought, doing the same.

"So this is a start-up screen?" she asked.

"Precisely." Back to business. "This is what you'll see each morning when you turn on the computer. We'll label the boxes under the logo with the various system components we create and you'll touch them or click on them with the mouse to go to, say, payroll or menu."

"Okay." She nodded.

"What I suggest we do next is go over each of the areas one by one. I'll design everything to your specifications, then we'll go into test phase, looking for things that don't work, or changes you'd like to make. Sound good?"

"Sounds great."

The serious work began then, and after much intensive talking, brainstorming and studying screens, Ryan felt he'd gathered enough information from Penny to lay out preliminary designs for the accounts payable and accounts receivable sections of the system.

As Penny leaned back in her chair next to him, he glanced toward the antique-looking clock on her mantel to see that it was already five-thirty.

"Time to call it a day?" she asked.

"Well," he admitted with a grin, "I haven't exactly been following normal business hours lately, so if I knock off this early, I'll feel like I'm really slacking. I'll probably head home and get back to work, start getting some of this information keyed into the laptop."

Penny gave him a derisive look. "Don't tell me, you're one of those guys who burns the midnight oil and never takes time to stop and smell the roses."

He shrugged. "Looks like you're onto me."

"That's bad for your health, you know. And I know your type. I bet my sandwiches are the healthiest food you've been putting into your body lately. Am I right?"

"Okay, you caught me again. I've had a standing late-night date with the girl at the McDonald's drive-through for the past week. But when you're in a competitive market and you want to get ahead, you've gotta give a hundred percent."

"Sure, but you don't have a hundred percent to give if you never stop to refuel." She shifted her gaze toward the kitchen. "Me, I'm gonna heat up some pot roast. *Real* food," she added teasingly.

"Wow, pot roast. I haven't had anything that good in ages." He winced inwardly as soon as he'd spoken, though—he hadn't meant to sound as if he was hinting for an invitation.

Penny's reply affirmed his fears. "I have plenty. I made dinner for my parents and sister yesterday, but I'll never be able to eat all the leftovers myself."

He shook his head. "Thanks, but no. I'm really anxious to get to work on this. I want to have some fresh screens to show you before we meet tomorrow afternoon." *And I also want to make sure we keep this just business.* The afternoon had gone surprisingly well and Ryan hated to risk screwing it up now by changing it into something social.

"I really don't mind. I can heat it up in the microwave and bake a couple of potatoes while I'm at it. It'll take fifteen minutes. And it's the least I can do, considering all the overtime you're planning to put in on this job. Unless..." she added, cringing slightly, "you think eating together would be too..."

"No," he said. "It's not that." Which was a lie, of course. He definitely thought it would be too awkward—maybe even tempting?—but he certainly couldn't admit it. Besides, maybe Penny was right; maybe he needed a little downtime if he was going to keep doing worthwhile work. He'd kept his professional wits about him all afternoon, so surely he could handle another hour in her presence. "Okay," he finally conceded, summoning a smile. "I'd love some real food."

When he offered to help, Penny assigned him the job of setting the small table in the breakfast nook that jutted off from the old-fashioned white-on-white kitchen. "Very retro," he said appreciatively of the white Formica table.

"Very garage sale." She laughed as she dug in the refrigerator, which also looked as though it had a few miles on it. "I like old things," she added, turning toward him, a large bowl covered with plastic wrap cradled in her arms. "I love these old hardwood floors and the old wooden cabinets. I bought this house with the idea of remodeling it, but by the time the restaurant was doing well enough that I could afford it, I'd grown attached to it all, just the way it is."

He found himself looking at her face then, seeing her features more clearly than ever before, concentrating on her perky nose, her easy smile. He smiled back, but then he stopped, because it was the smart thing to do.

He set out the aqua Fiestaware plates she'd handed to him, then rummaged in her drawers until he found silverware. Before, he'd only been vaguely aware of the vintage qualities of everything in her house, but now that it had been drawn to his attention, he concentrated on it, and he thought it was very Penny—simple, no-nonsense, yet full of an unnamable appeal.

Then, of course, he remembered that she wasn't as simple as he'd originally assumed. But outwardly, the Penny most of the world knew, and the Penny he was *supposed* to see, indeed fit with the home she'd chosen. He couldn't deny feeling comfortable there.

A few minutes later, they sat down together at the table. "This is great," he said, savoring each bite of pot roast he put in his mouth. "I don't think I've had this since I lived at home."

"Really?" Her eyes widened. "I don't think I could live without home-cooking. It's hard to cook for just myself, but I try to as much as possible."

"Is that why you opened a restaurant?"

She shrugged. "Partly. But I'll admit Patti and I were also thinking of money. We chose the pub atmosphere and downtown location with that in mind, and it's paid off. And our menu doesn't have much home-cooking on it—mostly sandwiches and a few soups—but I'm fond of food in general, I suppose. I like making it, and I like eating it."

Ryan laughed, thinking her terribly cute. He noticed

that even though she wasn't a pound overweight, she also wasn't sporting that skinny-as-a-stick look girls seemed to find so attractive these days. "I like a woman who eats," he confided in her. "A lot of the girls I've dated recently are the types who order a salad, no dressing, then watch me eat a huge steak. It makes for a pretty boring meal. I like to eat *with* someone."

Penny grinned. "I know what you mean. I don't mind eating alone, but if I'm sharing a meal with somebody, I want to really share the meal."

Ryan nodded his agreement, surprised she actually understood what he was talking about, since he'd never really thought about it before.

"So what brings you to Cincinnati from a bustling place like Chicago?"

"Just felt like I needed a new start," he said, keeping it simple. It was one thing to confide your eating quirks to someone, but another entirely to admit a history of job failures, especially considering the circumstances of their own relationship so far. "Martin made me a good offer and I liked what I saw in the company."

Penny nodded, and Ryan was sure he'd just imagined her disconcerted look at the mention of Martin's name. "Martin's a good boss, and a good businessman. I'm sure you'll be very happy with him."

"Can I ask you something?" he asked, after a moment. Part of him knew he shouldn't keep taking them back to that night, yet they were getting along so well he didn't think it was unreasonable to seek clarification on this.

She looked a little worried, but said, "Okay."

"About you and Martin. Did you, uh, tell me you were engaged? I...missed some of the details when we were discussing it."

Penny pushed back a lock of stray hair, dropped her gaze, then said, "No, we're not engaged, at least not yet. He's proposed, but I haven't given him an answer."

He nodded. "I see." He'd thought that was what she'd said, but hadn't been sure, and he'd wanted to know how deeply he'd encroached.

"And speaking of Martin, that reminds me—" she lifted one finger to her bottom lip "—he once showed me a program for another restaurant that had this nifty feature where you click on the item someone orders and all the little options pop up beside it, so no matter what someone wants or doesn't want on their food, the server doesn't have to let anyone know anything special because it's all right there in the extra menus." Then her pretty laughter washed over him. "Do you have any idea at all what I'm talking about?"

Swallowing the bite of baked potato in his mouth, he grinned. "Believe it or not, I do. It's a pop-up option box that displays a list of all the possible choices. There are several ways it can be programmed, and I've got some templates for it loaded on the laptop, so I can let you take a look at them before I leave."

"Great," she said, and they shared another smile.

Unfortunately, though, Ryan had the scary feeling that maybe these were getting to be more than just normal, professional smiles. Especially this one, because their gazes locked for a long time. He felt the connection in his gut, and he couldn't help noticing how deep the blue of her eyes shone in the dim lighting of the kitchen as the sun started dipping behind the trees outside.

"Well..." she said, suddenly sounding nervous again.

"Dinner was great," he said, taking over for her.

"Thanks a lot. Now I'd better show you those templates, then get out of your way for the evening."

He rose to his feet as Penny nodded in agreement, then wasted no time making his way back to the living room to his laptop. Taking a seat, he used the built-in mouse to maneuver his way to the windows he wanted to show her.

When she dropped into the chair next to him, he kept his eyes on the computer. "This screen shows the most common way to display the options," he said, then clicked to open another window, adding, "and this layout takes up less space on the monitor, but it's a little harder to see. There's a third method I personally like—" He reached to click the mouse again, but suddenly Penny's small hand came down soft on his.

His stomach clenched.

He swallowed and looked at her.

"Can you go back to the first option?" she asked. Yet when she saw his expression, she quickly drew back her hand as if realizing her error.

"Uh, yeah." His heart thumped like a seventh grader's who'd just been touched by a pretty girl. Eyes on the computer, he reopened the first window. "Sorry if I was going too fast."

"No, I just wanted to compare the two I've seen so far. Can this print be made smaller?" She reached across him to point at the monitor with one long, tapered finger, leaning closer than she had any time throughout the day.

"Not really." His senses began to swim with the fresh scent of her perfume. "Makes it too hard for the computer to distinguish which option is being selected with the screen-touch method," he continued, but he thought his voice sounded sort of strangled now.

"Ah," she said. And although she started to pull her arm back, she did it way too slowly...slow enough to give him time to wonder, to consider, to make the impulsive decision to reach up and gently catch her wrist in his hand.

Angling his body toward hers made it even clearer to Ryan how close they were to each other, how near her sweet eyes rested, and her soft lips, parted now in something that was either passion or surprise, he couldn't discern which. Time moved perilously slow. "I..." What? He what? "Oh, hell," he murmured, then leaned forward to brush a short but tantalizing kiss across her lips.

Penny nearly melted as the featherlight kiss swept through her. She hadn't expected it, but it had felt like a taste of heaven. Except for one thing. It was wrong. Wrong, wrong, wrong.

Yanking her arm away, she kicked her feet out to send her desk chair rolling across the room. *"What do you think you're doing?"*

"Kissing you?"

She couldn't believe he'd done it, no matter how nice it might've felt! "You can't be kissing me!"

Ryan nodded emphatically. "I know that, believe me."

"Then why did you do it?"

He gave a helpless sigh. "I have no idea."

The words left her even more stunned, only in a different way now, and she gasped, affronted, almost insulted. He was kissing her and he didn't even know why?

"What I mean is..."

"Yes?"

His demeanor shifted. "I have a lot to lose here, you know. Like my job."

"Then don't you think kissing me is a bad idea?"

"Absolutely." He suddenly looked determined, stalwart. "In fact, you're exactly the *last* type of woman I need in my life."

She pulled in her breath sharply. "What's that supposed to mean?"

"Well," he began, lifting his gaze to hers, "frankly, you're too wild for me."

Penny's mouth dropped open. What had just happened here? And how could he think…? Well, okay, she supposed he actually had every reason to think she was wild, but she'd hoped she'd succeeded in explaining all that away the other night in the limo. Apparently not. "Listen, I told you, that was just a onetime thing, a person I made up—"

"Sure, that's what you *told* me, but…"

She blinked in disbelief. "Are you calling me a liar?"

"I'm just saying…maybe you're a little wilder than you think you are."

"How would you know *what* I am?"

"Because you can't fake what we did together."

His answer hit Penny low and hard, and she struggled for a reply, feeling defensive now that his words hung in the air. "Well, you were just as wild back, and—and you didn't even think I was someone you knew! At least I *thought* I knew you."

"Well, *I'm* not the one denying I'm wild. I'll admit I have the capacity to be that way, but I can't because I came to Cincinnati to settle down and be a good boy."

"If you're such a good boy, then why did you respond in the limo?" Aha, Penny thought, she had him now.

But when their gazes met, she quit feeling defensive. His eyes were such a warm, alluring shade of brown and he looked...desperate, *passionate*.

"I couldn't resist," he finally admitted.

At least ten feet lay between them now. The fronds of a potted palm jutted in front of Penny's face. There seemed safety in distance, but his eyes were enough to melt her and she suddenly wished the limo hadn't been dark, that she'd had the pleasure of gazing into them as heatedly then as he gazed at her this moment.

"Can't now, either," he said, getting to his feet. He closed the distance between them before she could even think, let alone protest. He reached for her hand, pulled her up next to him, then lifted his palms to her face.

Don't. The word echoed inside her, but didn't make it to her lips. It was an automatic response, but not what she really wanted.

The kiss was as gentle and fleeting as the one just a minute ago, but this time Penny savored it and let the pleasure trickle warmly through her body. "Oh..." she breathed. "This isn't me."

"Yes, it is," he assured her, and she had no choice but to believe him when his next kiss came stronger, laced with the same thick desire she'd felt from him in the limo. She remembered the power, the restraint she'd felt in his kisses because she felt it now, too. And as she let herself get lost in the sensation of his mouth on hers, she longed to ask him to let go of that restraint and do everything to her.

"Your hair," he murmured in her ear as he sprinkled hot kisses just below. "It feels different than the other night."

Penny could barely find her voice. "I...curled it then."

"It feels so silky. And it smells so good. I thought it was your perfume, but it's your hair."

"Sh-shampoo," she managed, yet his breathy hot voice had turned her knees to jelly and she didn't want to talk anymore. Lifting one hand to his cheek, she led his mouth back to hers. As much as she loved being kissed other places, right now she needed to feel his magnificent kiss on her lips.

She'd never imagined such powerful chemistry could exist between two people, but it had the other night, even in the dark, and it pummeled her now, too, making her feel completely won, completely weakened, completely at his mercy.

That's when he pulled back, breaking away from her.

"Oh God," he said, his gaze planted behind her as things came to a grinding halt. "I'm sorry."

She followed his eyes to the desk, to the large vinyl portfolio Martin had given her to store her paperwork on the system design. The words Schuster Systems were emblazoned across it in bold gold lettering.

"It's okay," she said, trying to come to grips with all of this—his fabulous kisses, and the fact that, for both of their sakes, she should not have accepted them.

"No, it's not." He shook his head. "I can't do this."

"Neither can I."

"I shouldn't have. I don't mean to be a jerk."

She spoke quietly, gazing again into eyes she thought more beautiful each time she looked at them. "I don't think you're a jerk. I think we're just...in a weird situation." She paused, trying to clear her head. "We shouldn't be working together alone like this."

"I know, but how would we explain that to Martin?"

She glanced down. "That's the only reason I agreed to it—I couldn't figure out a way not to without looking suspicious." Raising her eyes back to him, she sighed. "But I think you should probably go now."

"Definitely."

Penny watched from the same spot where she'd stood kissing him a moment ago as he moved to the desk and hurriedly packed his laptop and the notes he'd taken during the day. Cramming it all in a leather bag, he strode to the front door, and only then did he stop to peer back at her.

"Penny," he said, looking desperate now, "I'm really sorry about kissing you. It was way out of line, weird situation or not. I just..." he sighed "...well, never mind."

I'm just so madly attracted to you I couldn't stop myself, Ryan had wanted to say, but no good could come from that much honesty. He couldn't believe what he'd done, how much more difficult he'd just made things for both of them. What had he been thinking? But then, that was the whole problem—he hadn't been thinking, he'd been *reacting.* To her. To everything about her. Damn his impulses.

"I'll see you tomorrow," he went on. "That is, if you still want to work with me on this project. Because if you don't, I'll figure out some other way, some reason I can't do it."

Penny shook her head. "No, I...actually think we work well together...when we're not kissing."

She looked nervous, but he reassured her. "So do I." It was the truth. "Good night," he said a little more brusquely than he'd intended as he headed out the door and proceeded down the front walk toward the curb, where he'd parked.

Pausing on the sidewalk, he looked over his shoulder to find Penny peering at him from inside the screen door. "One last thing," he said, feeling bolder than he had a right to.

"What's that?"

"Are you gonna marry him?" It was presumptuous as hell, but he had to know.

Behind the screen, she hesitated, and Ryan felt his heart balancing precariously on her answer.

"No," she finally admitted in little more than a whisper. "Of course not. How could I now?"

A flood of relief washed through him. "Good," he said. Then he turned to walk on, taking a full two steps before he stopped and looked back again. "But that still doesn't change things between us. Because Martin's still my boss and you're still too wild for me." He'd just wanted to make sure they both knew where they stood.

"Hey, you're the one who keeps kissing me. All you have to do is stop."

"Right." He nodded. "And I will."

Still, even as he slid behind the wheel of his car, started the engine and drove down the street, even as he reminded himself what was smart and right and rational, Ryan couldn't help feeling inexplicably happy that Penny was no longer tied to another man.

4

THE GREEN AWNINGS beyond the plate-glass windows shaded the sidewalk from the scorching midday sun. The lunch rush had ended not long ago and Penny heard the sounds of dishes being washed in the pub's kitchen.

She wiped down the bar, then glanced at the clock. Ryan was probably upstairs finishing his sandwich right now, probably still working in Martin's corner office, too. Thankfully, Grace had been at her desk when Penny had dropped the lunches off today, which had kept her from having to hang around the place. But whether or not she bumped into Ryan at Schuster Systems didn't really matter since he would be showing up at her house again in about an hour. She drew in a deep breath, then let it slowly back out, wishing she didn't feel so twitchy inside just thinking about him and all that had happened.

She kept reliving the moment when he'd brushed that impossibly soft kiss across her lips. It had melted through her like the thrilling purity of a first kiss, like first love, as if she were sixteen and untouched and waiting for that first magical taste of romance. Every time she thought about it, she felt his mouth grazing hers again. But it would probably be wise to stop thinking about it because— Oh, poor Martin!

She hadn't known what to do about Martin until the

words had left her yesterday. She wouldn't marry him. Couldn't marry him. Never even should have *considered* marrying him. She guessed being proposed to by a successful businessman, who was truly a nice person on top of it, had been flattering, and it had at least seemed worthy of some thought. But now any delusions of compatibility she'd been suffering had come to an end and she knew—

The rattle of a cup cut into her thoughts. *"Miss?"*

She looked up to find their last remaining lunch customer, a middle-aged businessman with messy hair and a wrinkled suit, waving his coffee cup at her from the end of the bar.

"Yes?"

"I *said*, can I get a refill down here?" His dark eyebrows knit and his expression reminded Penny of an angry bear.

She was stunned she'd let his cup go empty and had apparently been ignoring him, too. She always put customers first. Well, except for now, darn it. "Of course. I'm sorry." As she grabbed the coffeepot and scurried toward him, she could feel Patti's scowl from where she sat at a nearby table rolling silverware into napkins.

Great, now the whole Ryan/Martin fiasco was distracting Penny from her job, too. Still, thank God she'd figured out the right answer to Martin's proposal before it was too late.

So it was actually good this whole thing happened, she tried to convince herself, returning the coffeepot to its place. Wanting another guy so much had made the decision about marrying Martin clearer than anything else could have. But now her entanglement with Ryan was over because of his job. Which was also good, because even after she officially broke things off with

Martin, it would look awfully suspicious if she and Ryan were suddenly together, wouldn't it? And besides, he had the ridiculous idea that she was too wild for him anyway. "Ha!"

"What?" Patti looked up, clearly perplexed. Penny felt the rumpled businessman's questioning gaze, as well.

"Nothing." She shook her head lightly. She'd not meant to say that aloud, but when she thought about Ryan's accusation, it made her a little crazy inside.

After all, she'd been accused of a lot of things in her day. In elementary school, she'd been called Goody Two-Shoes; in junior high, she'd been the Teacher's Pet; and in high school, she'd not dated a lot due to her reputation as a Nice Girl. Her family and friends had always labeled her with words like *dependable* and *hardworking*, and Patti always distinguished between the two of them by calling her The Sweet One. But no one had ever, by any stretch of the imagination, called Penny Halloran *wild*.

On the other hand, she chided herself, you did seduce the man in a limousine. The same man with whom she had to design a computer system now. The same man she couldn't kiss anymore, or have sex with anymore, either. She shook her head in disbelief, then tossed down her rag. The whole thing still didn't quite seem real, and her confusion over it had escalated with Ryan's kisses last night.

Finishing up a few last tasks behind the bar, Penny took a look around. After asking one of the waitresses, Lisa, to refill ketchup bottles when she got a chance, she said to Patti, "I've gotta run. Ryan will be over soon."

"Oh yeah. Time for your big computer date."

Penny blinked and hoped she looked normal. "What

are you talking about?" It didn't help that Lisa and Bearface down at the end of the bar were both listening, too.

"I'm not sure," Patti said, sounding irritatingly sleuthlike, "but I'm telling you, you get wide-eyed and sort of...aloof whenever you mention him."

Great, so she *didn't* look normal. "Do not," she protested. And she was arguing like a seven-year-old on top of it.

"Whatever you say," Patti replied in a singsong voice that told Penny her sister wasn't buying it. She got the idea Patti thought Ryan was a better choice for her than Martin even without knowing him.

If only she could keep Martin on her mind for half as long as she thought about Ryan, maybe she wouldn't feel like such a rotten person. She dreaded turning down Martin's proposal, but once she did—and once she got through this system design with Ryan—this would all be over.

And as for the little stab of pain in her chest when she thought of things with Ryan being over...well, Penny never had been particularly skilled at the art of casual dating. So it probably stood to reason that having sex with someone would cause some odd, jarring feelings of infatuation. She guessed that was what you'd call it, and she was a tad disconcerted that it seemed to be getting steadily worse.

But a little—or even a lot—of infatuation didn't matter. It *couldn't* matter. Ryan had made it clear that whatever attraction he felt for her wasn't enough to make him throw away his new job, and she couldn't blame him. After all, they barely knew each other.

Penny glanced toward the bearfaced man to find him looking amused by her discussion with Patti. "She's completely mistaken," she said. Then, mumbling a quick goodbye to Patti, she snatched up her purse and exited the restaurant before her sister could get any wiser that there was more to this story than met the eye.

RYAN TOOK A DEEP BREATH as he approached Penny's front door. It felt dangerous, as if he were returning to the scene of a crime. He still couldn't believe he'd made such a lunkhead move yesterday. No wonder he kept losing jobs—he kept letting his wants get in the way of his responsibilities. What would it take before he learned his lesson? Another job loss? Another relocation? Maybe he'd never get it figured out and go broke in the process. As for whatever insane sense of relief he'd felt driving away from her house last night, he'd decided it only had to do with her decision about Martin easing his guilt a little, making him feel a bit less like a trespasser. Because he'd meant what he'd said, she was too intense for him. And he couldn't keep screwing up every job he got, every chance someone gave him to build a career. So that meant...

You cannot think about her black bra. You cannot think about her slender curves. You can't even think about how soft her lips were yesterday or the pretty scent of her hair.

"Hi," Penny said, opening the door just as he was about to knock. "How are you?" Her eyes sparkled with a surprisingly friendly welcome and her lips looked horribly silken and inviting, which made it difficult not to think about them. And, damn it, her hair still smelled that way. What was it, some kind of flower or fruit? He almost asked on impulse, when he jolted himself to a halt.

"I think it would be smart," he said on an exhale, "for us to skip the small talk and get right to work."

She looked surprised, perhaps irritated, even as her warm blue eyes took on that ridiculously innocent quality he'd noticed before. Yet she caught her breath and said, "Whatever you think is best."

Heading for her desk, he took a seat and set up his laptop, staying focused on the hardware in front of him.

"Something to drink?" she asked. "Not that I mean to make small talk. But it's hot outside and I thought you might be parched."

He resisted the urge to glance up at her, instead watching his computer screen blink to life. Still, from his peripheral vision, he saw she wore her usual khaki shorts and a white sleeveless blouse, and her hair was knotted up on top of her head in some sort of clip. A glimpse down revealed that her feet were bare, which struck him as adorably sexy, although he had no idea why and absolutely refused to think about it. "No thanks," he said.

Did she just roll her eyes at him? He couldn't tell for sure, since he wasn't looking directly at her, but he could've sworn... "Did you just roll your eyes at me?" he asked, swinging his gaze onto hers.

Big mistake. When their eyes met, he felt it in his gut.

"As a matter of fact—" she planted her fists on her hips "—I did."

His heartbeat rose to his throat, but he merely lifted his eyebrows in question.

"Look, I understand the need to keep this all about business, but don't you think you're being a little extreme?"

"Nope, just ready to get to work," he claimed, forcing a smile, one of those professional ones that had come a little easier yesterday. He motioned to the laptop. "I want to show you the screens I put together last night."

When she slid into the chair next to his, finally allowing them to get Day Two of the project under way, Ryan exhaled a sigh of relief, then pointed to the laptop with a pen. "Okay, you recall the start-up screen. Now, when you click on the Accounting box—" he demonstrated "—you'll be asked for a password."

Together, they set up a password for Penny to use during the test phase, and she chose "prettypenny," explaining with a wistful smile that her grandpa had called her that when she was a little girl. "He and my grandmother had a farm down in Kentucky, about an hour south of here. The land is covered with strip malls and fast food restaurants now, but back then, there was a silo, and acres of tall corn, and a tire swing that hung from the big apple tree in front of their house, just for Patti and me."

Ryan himself had grown up in a rural farming community, and though Penny's memories of such surroundings sounded warmer than his own, it reminded him of good times. "My brother Dan and I had a swing, too, a wooden one. My dad sat down in it one day after we'd outgrown it and broke right through it."

They shared a smile over Ryan's recollection, and he decided he certainly agreed with her grandfather's nickname for her, but how had they gotten off track so quickly? He determinedly wiped the grin from his face and returned his eyes to the computer, ready to move into the accounting program once and for all.

An incredible sense of relief washed over him as he finally fell into full work mode, soon showing her the accounting elements he'd designed for the pub after leaving last night. He supposed his comfort came from having done this hundreds of times; working with clients had become second nature to him and explanations for each screen display rolled off his tongue with ease. But he didn't really care why, he only cared that it'd happened, that she hadn't distracted him with any more personal stuff, and that he'd finally started acting more professionally before anything could go awry.

Every now and then, Penny uttered an "mmm-hmm" or an "ah" or asked a question, and he made sure she understood the relevant features of each component before going to the next. Periodically, he asked her to give suggestions or point out things she disliked, taking notes and responding with suggestions of his own. By the time they'd walked through the screens he'd created, he felt a familiar sense of pride and satisfaction in his work.

"All right then," he said, "we've got the payables and receivables programs roughed in, let's move on to payroll. Like yesterday, I'll want to look at your notes, hear your thoughts, and we'll discuss ideas and look at some templates."

Glancing up, he saw her smile. "Dare I suggest a bathroom break?"

Ryan leaned back in his chair with a sigh and slowly let a conceding grin spread across his face. "I guess that's not a *totally* unreasonable request."

"And I, for one, am thirsty. Sure I can't tempt you?" She raised her eyebrows.

Okay, maybe he *had* been a little rigid earlier—it was easier to see in retrospect. But now they'd proven this could still be done, they could still work together like two normal human beings, two mature adults, even after last evening's kisses. "All right. I'll have something cold."

Penny got to her feet and padded from the room, and he had to admit, things truly seemed ordinary here. They were working well together as they had the other day, making good progress, and he was enjoying the interaction the same way he usually enjoyed client interaction. He might catch the occasional whiff of her hair now and then—what *was* that fragrance?—and he might notice the cute lilt in her voice when she caught on to how something worked, but overall, they'd fallen back into the roles of client and system designer with startling ease.

"I made some lemonade before you got here," her voice echoed from the kitchen.

"Sounds great." Peering at her hard drive resting upright on the floor beneath the desk, Ryan shrugged free of his suit jacket and got down on his knees. He started fiddling with the floppy drive where, sure enough, a diskette was lodged inside. It surprised him Martin couldn't have spent a little time making Penny's computer functional, but tomorrow, he'd bring a tool kit and take a closer look.

"It's from my grandma's secret recipe," she called, still in the other room.

"Your grandma has a secret recipe for lemonade?" he yelled back. "How can there be a secret to that?"

He continued to poke and prod at the diskette as she replied. "If I told you, it wouldn't be a secret, would it?"

Her playful tone made him smile. "Is this the same grandma who lived in Kentucky?"

"Yep, same one."

"So you said the farm isn't a farm anymore. Did *all* the Hallorans get into the food-and-drink business?"

"No, just Patti and me. My father owns a hardware store, one of the last family-run ones in the city. And my grandparents are retired. But they probably *should* all be in the restaurant business. My grandmother and mother are wonderful cooks and they taught me everything I know."

"What about Patti?" he asked over his shoulder. "They didn't teach her?"

Penny's short laugh resonated through the house. "Well, they tried, but it didn't work out. She handles more the management end of the business, the hiring, the firing, the banking. And I handle the menu and payroll...and now, I guess, the computer."

The glasses nearly slipped from Penny's hands when she entered the room to see Ryan down on all fours, his suit-clad butt in the air. She'd never really seen his butt before, but it looked nice. Really nice. Pinpricks of sensation skittered up her inner thighs. Right when things were going so smoothly, too.

After standing frozen in place for a moment, she lowered the two lemonades quietly to the corner of the desk, then headed for the bathroom. That's why she'd originally gotten up, wasn't it? And she certainly didn't want to get caught gaping, or risk messing up what had, so far, been a nice, normal workday between them, despite what she'd felt upon his arrival. Familiar tendrils of desire had curled through her when she'd found him standing on her doorstep looking totally *GQ*, but she'd pushed them down, helped along by his brusque candor and his refusal to look at her. Now, however, the tension had eased—other than these sexy little shivers he never had to know about—and she hoped they could keep things on an even keel.

When she returned, Ryan had, thankfully, risen back to his chair to take a sip of lemonade. "This is good."

But their eyes met, and something warm melted through her. Uh-oh.

"Real lemons, ice not water, and lots of extra sugar," she unthinkingly blurted out, then hurried to take her seat beside him. Somehow it was easier then, when they were looking at the computers and not each other.

"What?" he asked.

She lifted her gaze, then lowered it just as quickly. "That's the recipe. In case you wanted to know."

Maybe he'd been right when he'd arrived, Penny thought. Maybe anything else *was* inviting trouble. Reaching for her own lemonade, she took a long swallow and tried to let it cool her down inside.

She felt his glance from the corner of her eye. "I thought it was a secret."

Penny sighed. "Well, you seem trustworthy," she said, for lack of any better response.

He reached to type something onto his laptop and accidentally bumped her arm. They both flinched uncomfortably, then exchanged lightning-quick looks.

"So..." he said.

"So..." she replied. Her heart beat too fast. Darn it, why couldn't they act normal around each other for longer periods of time?

"Let's talk payroll," he suggested hurriedly.

"Yes, let's."

WHEN RYAN LOOKED past her toward the window, Penny raised her gaze, as well.

"It's getting dark," he said.

It startled Penny to see dusk falling outside; the lights she'd turned on this afternoon had kept them from noticing the gradual change. She glanced to the mantel clock. "I can't believe it's so late. Almost nine."

He gave his head a regretful shake. "My fault. I get on a roll, and I totally lose track of time."

"No need to apologize," Penny assured him. "I'm just surprised. I had no idea we'd worked that long." But when she thought about it, they'd covered a lot. They'd gone over her manual payroll procedures and discussed how to best represent them in the system, then they'd moved on to her notes about budget and the monthly balance sheets. Although the comfort level had grown steadily deeper, Penny had remained aware of her attraction to him.

Now Ryan's smile trickled through her like a hot drink. "It's always a good sign when time flies, you know. Every now and then, I get into a situation where it's just the opposite, where one hour with a client feels like five, and that always means we're getting nothing accomplished. But I feel really positive about our work here, and I think we'll create a system you'll like."

So it would seem Ryan really had relaxed now. He could smile at her without panicking. Which meant she was the only one here still feeling...things. Tingly, ripply, urgelike things.

But that's good, she told herself. Heartbreaking in a way, since it was always nice to think a guy wanted you, but hadn't she decided for his sake, and for Martin's sake, that Ryan was right and nothing more could happen between them? She made herself smile back, glad—in theory anyway—that things felt more normal again as it did when they were both buried in work.

Yet did she just sense some slight, barely perceptible change in the air? No, probably not. It was likely just wishful thinking on her body's part. The little thrill that had zipped down through her when they'd shifted their gazes from the computer to one another just now probably meant nothing. The fact that Ryan's eyes, now squarely planted on hers, seemed to be filling with something like heat was probably entirely in her imagination.

"Can I offer you dinner?" She regretted the invitation even as it left her, but it'd just popped out. She rushed ahead, anxious to fill the suddenly awkward moment with more words. "Usually, I would've eaten hours ago. If you don't mind more pot roast, I could make some sandwiches with it. Or if you're ready to take off, that's fine, too. Whatever you want."

She actually thought he looked tempted, until he said, "Thanks, but I should definitely get going."

Penny simply nodded. Definitely, he'd said. The conviction in his voice brought her down to earth, and considering what had happened last night after eating together, she couldn't argue with his unspoken logic.

He drew his eyes away as he shut down his laptop. "Can I ask you something before I go, though?"

"Okay."

"I was wondering...how you're doing over the Martin thing. Your decision not to marry him, I mean."

"Oh." The question startled her, though she hardly knew why since Martin's proposal had been the entire basis of their bizarre relationship so far. "I'm doing fine."

So fine, in fact, that I keep wanting you. She didn't know if it was the dusky lighting and the falling of night, or if it was simply the culmination of urges she'd been battling all day, but as her desires escalated, this seemed like a good time to put some distance between them. She left the desk and moved casually to her overstuffed couch. That way she couldn't do something crazy like touch him if the unstoppable urge arose. Especially now that he seemed so in control, so totally uninterested in her physically. Nothing would be worse than making a move and getting rejected.

"When are you going to tell him?" Ryan asked, slipping the laptop in its case.

"Whenever he calls from Vegas." And, actually, she was surprised she hadn't heard from Martin yet—it was Tuesday and he'd left on Friday. She'd expected a call over the weekend, but at least the delay had given her time to work on what she was going to say.

"You're going to tell him over the phone?" Ryan asked, turning his chair to face her. It didn't sound like an accusation, just an honest question.

Penny took a deep breath before replying. "This way, he won't have to break down in front of me, you know? And I'd rather get it over with, not put it off."

Ryan's gaze focused directly on her now, unnervingly so. "I'm sorry, Penny, if I ruined something good between the two of you."

Her stomach dropped. It had never even occurred to her that Ryan didn't know the very brief history she shared with Martin, or how unexpected his proposal had been. "You didn't." She shook her head emphatically. "We'd only been dating a few months."

He shrugged. "It doesn't always take months to have a serious relationship. It happens all the time. People meet and fall in love like *that*." He snapped his fingers.

And she wondered, for the first time, about Ryan's love life. "Has that ever happened to you?"

"Me? No." He shook his head almost as if the idea were preposterous, even though he'd brought it up himself. "I *know* people who it's happened to, but I'm not sure I could ever fall in love that quickly myself."

"Why?" His comment perplexed her, and somewhere deep inside, she was a little hurt. Maybe she'd hoped this sensual energy between them was about more than sex, that he was harboring some secret, budding affection for her that he just hadn't had the courage to mention.

He raised his gaze, as if confiding in her. "I guess maybe I'm just cautious."

Did that mean he'd been hurt before? "Bad relationships in the past?" she ventured.

Ryan shook his head. "Nothing like that." He smiled slightly, his expression turning mischievous. "Maybe cautious is the wrong word. Maybe it's more like... reluctant. There's nothing too heavy in my past, and I guess I like it that way. I like keeping things light and being on my own at the end of the day, if you know what I mean."

Yes, she knew exactly what he meant. He wasn't looking for a relationship. He'd told her he'd come here to be a good boy, that he didn't want anything wild in his life, so apparently women were on the back burner for him completely right now. Or he wanted them to be, anyway. Because, there was, of course, her, and what had happened, and what, she supposed uncertainly, could *still* happen....

Oh, darn it, that proved it; she really *did* still want him. Desire hummed through her veins even as she sat talking with him. "Well, despite what you may think, things were very casual between me and Martin. And the truth is, I didn't know him all that well, romantically speaking."

Ryan tilted his head. "But in the limo..."

"Yes?"

"Well, you didn't seem shy."

Penny tried to swallow her embarrassment, but

failed. And considering how many personal details Ryan knew about her already, she saw no reason not to explain this, as well. "As I said that night, I wanted to find out if Martin had a wild side, too."

When she least expected it, a slow, almost wicked smile unfurled across Ryan's face.

"What?" she asked in response.

"So you admit it. You *are* wild."

Penny released a long, exasperated sigh. "I admitted I have a wild *side.* That's different than being wild."

"You said you were living out a fantasy," Ryan reminded her.

"So? Everyone has fantasies."

"But—" he raised one finger in the air "—not everyone lives them out."

Penny drew in her breath, wishing she could break her gaze with his, wishing she wanted to. But his unexpected words were settling deep inside her, easing their way into cracks and crevices she'd never peered into before.

Oh God, it was true. She'd read enough articles in *Cosmo* and *Glamour* to know most people—women anyway—never did attempt to live out their fantasies. Most women probably kept them inside and saw them as impossibilities, even as things they didn't truly want to happen. But the moment Penny had started exploring hers, she'd known she really wanted them to take place. They were experiences she truly desired, adventures she intended to have. And her own thoughts a moment ago only seemed to confirm it; she'd been sitting there wanting Ryan even though she knew that *he* couldn't let it happen, and *she* couldn't let it happen, and that it was all wrong.

Suddenly feeling as transparent as a negligee, she

thrust herself up from the couch and walked across the room toward the foyer, anxious to escape his gaze. She had no reply to what he'd just said, but it was as if he'd just shone a flashlight into the darkest corner of her soul. Coming to a stop before the mirror near the door, she fumbled for something to do with her hands, some way to distract herself from the nervous tension swirling through her. She adjusted the leaves of a philodendron spilling from a pot on a shelf next to the mirror, then reached below, turning on the stereo.

The low sounds of Marvin Gaye singing "Let's Get It On" wafted through the room.

She bit her lip. This probably wasn't a good moment for the sexiest song of all time, yet for some reason, she couldn't bring herself to change it.

That meant nothing, though. It didn't mean she was wild, nor did it mean she was waiting for something to happen here. She just didn't want to look panicky, that was all. She didn't want to do anything to let him know how tense and how...utterly *sexual* she suddenly felt.

And if she really *were* wild, wouldn't she start swaying her hips back and forth to the music, or stripping to it? As it was, she clamped both hands to the shelf supporting the stereo and held on for dear life, lest she faint from nervousness. Hardly the act of a wanton woman.

"I know about the limo now—" Ryan's voice came from behind her, low and sexy and *close* "—but what other kinds of fantasies do you have, Penny?"

She lifted her gaze to the mirror to find him standing behind her. His eyes burned with everything she felt, that same desire, that same undeniable want. One defensive part of her wished she could tell him he'd just crossed a line by asking her something so deeply personal, but considering what they'd done together in the limo, and that she'd told him it was a fantasy come true, she didn't really think he had. And she wished she were more offended by his forwardness, but nothing with Ryan ever felt wrong. Not from that first touch, that first kiss. It was a startling revelation. Everything she did with him always felt good and right and meant to be, no matter how much they both knew it shouldn't happen.

She should've been asking him what he thought he was doing, reminding him of his own rules. Instead, though, she skipped ahead to something that came from deeper inside, a fact she needed to make clear to him once and for all. "Take a good look at me, Ryan," she said, peering at him in the mirror. "I'm the girl next door. The teacher's pet. I'm June Cleaver and Mary Tyler Moore and all the Waltons rolled into one." She spread her arms helplessly. "I am *not* wild."

Never letting his eyes leave hers, Ryan reached up and pulled the clip from her hair, letting it fall down her back in a rush. Then, placing his hands on her shoulders, he gently turned her to face him. Without pause, his fingers moved to the buttons on her blouse, where he undid one, then the next, then the next. Penny tried to make herself protest, step away from him, anything, but her skin tingled with too much pleasure. *I am not wild, I am not wild,* she whispered silently. Yet her body didn't seem to agree with her at the moment.

"Maybe you're not wild on the outside," he said, his voice husky. "But underneath..."

As Ryan freed the last button on her blouse, he pushed it open to reveal a lacy lavender bra. The sight stole his breath and proved his point better than anything he could've said. Who'd have thought Penny the Sandwich Girl would wear *this* under her simple shirts?

Then he remembered the other night, the sexy black

lace beneath his fingertips. And when he put that whole experience together with this discovery, he knew without doubt that everything he'd said about her was true—she was wild at heart. It went deeper than one night, deeper than one fantasy, and maybe she didn't know it, but he did. Nothing he'd ever done had felt sexier than pushing the blouse from her shoulders, unveiling the sensual woman beneath the facade of simplicity.

Tracing one fingertip down the lavender strap of her bra, he followed the seam over the rounded ridge of her breast to the center where a tiny bow connected the cups. "You're so bad for me," he whispered.

Her voice trembled. "I see it the other way around."

Part of him wanted to argue, to remind her that her commitment to Martin was over and she no longer had anything to lose, whereas he still had everything at stake. He wanted to tell her just how good for her he could be, how he could prove to her how unrestrained she was, if only his job didn't stand in the way. But he feared any words he spoke would bring this moment to a screeching halt.

And even though he knew he was committing career suicide, he was like an addict who couldn't see reason, who only wanted one more taste of her, one more touch. The longer he was with her, the longer they'd talked—be it about work or families or the little asides she'd shared from time to time about her neighborhood or the hot weather—the more desire had begun to build inside him. He liked her. He liked her laughter. He liked the innocence that draped so honestly over her sensuous side. He liked that she was smart and talented, which showed in the way she ran her business, yet she was equally genuine and down-to-earth, making the same lemonade her grandmother did. And he also liked her wild side, which had caused something else to gather in him without his quite knowing it, too— a compulsion, a driving need, to free her sensuality beneath his hands.

Lowering his hands to her slender waist, Ryan deftly unbuttoned her shorts, then slid down the zipper. He watched his fingers working, but heard her breathing. He wanted to do this gradually, leisurely, wanted to rediscover that slow, intense heat they'd shared in the limo, everything else be damned.

Dropping to his knees at her side as the music urged him on, he reached up to ease the shorts over her hips. She gazed down, biting her lip in what he read as sweet, sexy surrender, and gently wriggled free of them. The motion turned his knees to mush, especially when he discovered the matching lavender thong she wore beneath, the lacy elastic disappearing down the center of her rounded bottom.

This woman didn't know how incredibly hot she was? It seemed impossible, but Ryan felt bound and determined to show her, to make her know it, just as *he* did.

Bending forward, he placed a feathery kiss on her bared hip and listened as she pulled in her breath. Shifting slightly, he lowered another tender kiss to her rear, and then another. His chest tightened as his desire wound tighter and hotter. She arched her backside toward him and he glanced up to see her arms raised over her head as if she were some sensual statue. He rained more soft kisses across her perfect bottom, and her sexy sighs drowned out the music altogether until all Ryan knew was her body, her sounds, her scent, the sensuality that almost dripped from her.

"You're so incredible," he breathed.

"I...I don't do these things." she whispered from above. Just as he'd feared, he should've stayed quiet.

"It's okay, Penny," he said soothingly, nibbling around the thin strip of lavender at her waist. "If you're still afraid I'll think badly of you, I won't, I swear. We're both human."

"It's not that. It's just that...I really *don't* do these things. Not without knowing a guy. And even then..." she moaned when he moved his kisses to the other side of her rear "...it's not like this."

"What do you mean?"

"No man has ever...undressed me in my foyer and started kissing me this way."

He leaned forward to place a kiss at the small of her back that made her gasp, yearning to make her understand what was going on inside her, yearning to help her release it. "Then why are you doing these things with *me?*"

She gazed over her shoulder, down into his eyes. "I guess it feels like I know you," she admitted. "I don't know why."

"I feel the same way," he told her. It was true. From the beginning.

"But we...don't. Not really."

"We're starting to. And I want to know you better."

"Yet there's still Martin to think about and—"

"Shh," he said, desperate not to let anything more interfere with the raging attraction he felt toward her. He hooked his thumbs gently into the elastic at her waist, his voice a mere growl. "Don't let any of that matter. Don't let it stop this."

At that precise second, the phone rang, and they both

flinched. "Damn it," Ryan groaned as the trilling noise sliced through his pleasure.

Penny gasped. "Maybe it's Martin."

He ground out a muttered curse.

She tripped free from the shorts at her ankles and took off toward the phone in the kitchen, as Ryan pushed to his feet, then shoved his hand back through his hair.

"Hello?" Penny quaked as she thrust the receiver beneath her ear. *Please don't let it be Martin.* She didn't think she could deal with that right now.

"Hey, what's up? You sound out of breath." It was Patti, thank God. But then, in a way, that was just as bad.

"I was just..." *About to have sex with a stranger for the second time in a week.* Oh dear, she really *had* been about to do that! Her! Good girl Penny Halloran! "I was just cleaning. I was...up to my elbows in suds and I ran to get the phone."

"You were cleaning? At nine o'clock on a Tuesday night?"

Penny really didn't think it sounded so preposterous. Some people cleaned at odd hours. "Is there some rule against that?"

"No, but I just think it's strange."

"Well, I want to get back to it, so did you call for some purpose?"

"I just wanted to tell you I'll be late tomorrow. I have a dentist's appointment I forgot about. But hey, far be it from me to interrupt a late-night cleaning frenzy, so I won't keep you."

Penny felt bad for lying to Patti so much lately, not to mention that her behavior must seem extremely suspicious. But considering she stood in the kitchen in her underwear and Ryan still waited for her in the foyer, she took the out. "Okay. See you tomorrow. Bye."

Hanging up, she drew a deep breath and glanced toward the doorway, girding herself for whatever would come next. She couldn't quite believe she was about to let this happen, and she didn't know where Penny the Sweet One had disappeared to, but she wanted this. Even with Patti's interruption, even with her fears that it had been Martin calling, her body still hummed with the passion it seemed only Ryan loosed in her. She bit her lip as she rounded the corner, suddenly feeling as wild and sexy as he kept telling her she was.

5

THE INSTANT Penny met Ryan's eyes, she knew everything had changed. He wore that torn expression she'd seen on his face before. He'd picked up her blouse and now held it out to her. She took it, painfully aware of the silence now filling the room; he'd turned the music off while she was away.

He lifted one hand to her cheek and his voice came low and deliberate. "I love the way you look right now, Penny. And I love how wild you are, even if you don't see it. But I have to go."

"Oh." She only hoped the hurt bubbling inside her didn't show.

"I like you so much; you don't know how much. But this is—"

"Wrong?" she supplied.

"Right," he said, meeting her eyes briefly before lowering his gaze. "I can't risk my job this way. I wish I could, but I can't."

"I understand," she replied, but her voice sounded hollow to her because she still wanted him to stay, still wanted things to be the way they were when they forgot about Martin and Schuster Systems. Suddenly feeling naked in her lavender underwear, she thrust her arms into her shirt, then held it closed in front.

Ryan moved to the desk to retrieve his laptop and jacket, then hurried back toward the door. He paused to lower a conciliatory kiss to her forehead as he passed by, but Penny hardly noticed, too stunned by how quickly things had shifted. A second later, the door shut behind him and she felt more alone than she had in a very long time.

She knew why he had to go; she knew it made sense. And earlier, she'd been all about trying to do the sensible thing, for the sake of his job, and for Martin's sake, too. But as she buttoned up her blouse, she still ached inside. As it turned out, there *was* something worse than making a move and getting shot down—having *him* make a move, then change his mind.

He'd left her on the night after they'd had sex in the limousine, and that had been fine. In fact, it had been the only reasonable thing about the entire evening. He'd left her again last night after the passionate kisses they'd shared and she'd still understood why it had to be, and that had strengthened her.

But tonight, everything was different. Maybe because she felt as though she really knew him. Maybe because of the reminder that he was aware of her fantasies; no one else knew those secrets and it built a certain, unplanned intimacy between them. Maybe because throughout the day, they had talked, shared things, and she'd started feeling comfortable with him, and she'd thought that mattered. Maybe the physical attraction she felt toward him, even the irrational sense of infatuation, was beginning to be *more.*

She sank into an easy chair and buried her head in her hands. An emotional attachment to this guy—a guy who worked for Martin—was the last thing she needed. Her insides twisted with knowing that when forced to make a choice between her and the job, he chose the latter.

And yet, what did she expect? Who was she to him? Nobody but a girl who had thrown herself into his lap in a dark car, ripped his clothes off and attacked him. How had she gotten herself into this mess?

Penny took a deep breath and rose to her feet. She wasn't going to think about this anymore; she couldn't right now. She had something more important to do, something which suddenly couldn't wait a moment longer.

She didn't know Martin's conference schedule, but she knew she wanted to get her loose ends with him tied up this very minute. At least then she'd feel a little less guilty. Things were messy enough without his proposal still hanging over her head.

He was staying at the Flamingo Hilton, so she called 411, got the number, and dialed furiously. "Martin Schuster's room please," she said to the nasal-sounding operator. As she waited, she walked with the cordless to the foyer and clumsily maneuvered back into her shorts, deciding the conversation would be easier without reminders that she'd just had her clothes off for someone else.

Settling on the couch, she tensed when the ringing abruptly ended, then took a deep, preparatory breath... only to hear a ridiculously pleasant-sounding female voice say, "The party you are trying to reach is unavailable. Please leave a message."

Martin, I'm sorry, but I just can't marry you. Penny opened her mouth to speak, then let out a huge sigh and hung up, every ounce of boldness evaporating. Telling him on the phone was one thing, but leaving it on an answering machine just wasn't human, no matter how desperate she was for closure.

"Oh, would you just call me, you idiot!"

Staring at the phone in her hand, Penny tried to get hold of herself. Her entire body still tingled with crazed mixtures of excitement and disappointment and anticipation and failure. She felt her eyes growing wet, but refused to cry, and when a tear rolled down her cheek, she obstinately wiped it away. Everything inside her felt crazy.

Eat, you need to eat. It was late and her blood sugar was probably low.

As she moved to the kitchen, still feeling defiant, Penny decided she'd had enough pot roast for one week. Given the unusual circumstances of the evening—and of her life lately—she was going to throw all dietary caution to the wind and indulge herself.

Grabbing a tray from the pantry, she loaded it up with horrible, wonderful things. A plate of brownies. A tub of French vanilla ice cream. A dish of strawberries and an extra large bowl of whipped cream.

Now, she told herself as she carried the tray to the bathroom, *calm down. Be good to yourself. Try to enjoy this. Try to feel like you again.* Normal Penny, who owned a business and behaved professionally at all times. Good Girl Penny, who didn't sleep with strangers. Pretty Penny, the Sweet One, the apple of her grandpa's eye. Yes, it would be good to get back on more familiar emotional ground.

The warm peach tones of the old-fashioned bathroom soothed her instantly as she balanced her tray on the rounded edge of the big claw-footed tub. That's why she'd chosen the color, to remind her of sunsets and seashells and the way the sun's warmth could lull you into total relaxation. Going to the old pedestal sink, Penny splashed cool water on her face, glad she'd conquered her tears, then poured a long stream of Sunny

Peach bubble bath beneath warm running water. Finding a scrunchy, she knotted her hair in it, then scurried to the foyer to turn the radio back on. The same station from earlier still played slow soul. She didn't bother changing it, though, concentrating on the song's tranquil rhythm.

When the tub was almost full, she turned off the water, slipped out of her clothes, then stepped into the luxurious bubbles. Sinking into the suds, she leaned her head back and let the music sedate her. She occasionally reached for a strawberry or brownie, dipping it in either the softening ice cream or the smooth whipped cream before putting it in her mouth.

As the sudsy water caressed her skin, however, the rich foods somehow heightened her sensual awareness. The sensations hardly brought back Normal Penny, but instead seemed to invite the newer, more daring version of herself she'd so recently uncovered.

After eating her fill of the sweets, she stretched out in the tub, sinking deeper into the moist bubbles, and let her mind begin to wander. She thought about Ryan and the foyer, although she refused to dwell on the hurt that still lingered, so instead she found herself imagining the things that might have happened if the phone hadn't rung. She even imagined placing a sexy call to Ryan, using her feminine wiles to somehow lure him back.

Then other outrageous pictures entered her head, more fantasies, some she was familiar with already, others that were brand-new. Just envisioning them somehow made her feel unfettered, free. Admittedly, none of this was doing much to lower her level of frustration, yet she couldn't stop her mind from exploring all the stirring new possibilities that floated through her thoughts.

And then she gasped, bolting upright in the tub and sloshing water over the edge.

Was it possible? Could it be true?

All these fantasies, running rampant in her head... The sexy undies she always wore, even though no one usually saw them... And she'd seduced a man in a limousine. She'd done that, really made it happen.

And, oh, the positively *wicked* things she wanted to do to Ryan, if only he would let her.

A sharp tingle whisked through her body, traveling from the top of her head to the tips of her fingers and toes, and Penny knew without doubt it really *was* true. Everything inside her pointed to it, and she couldn't believe she'd been so blind for so long. She could only assume this was something that had been buried deep inside her for years, and it was finally fighting its way free. She bit her lip at the stunning revelation that she didn't know herself at all...that she really *wasn't* such a good girl.

RYAN STOOD PEERING into his refrigerator, wishing he saw something to eat. Instead, he found beer, soda, orange juice and margarine. He'd stayed so busy at work that he hadn't even gotten unpacked yet, much less found time to make a serious trip to the grocery store. Closing one door and opening another, he explored the freezer with a little more success. He'd grabbed a box of pizza rolls and some frozen garlic bread at a convenience store the other night when he'd stopped for drinks. Turning on the oven, he found a pizza pan and emptied the contents of both packages onto it. Not exactly pot roast, but all things considered, it would do.

While the food was in the oven, Ryan shed his suit and tie, changing into a pair of old gym shorts and a

T-shirt. Moving back through the spacious yet bare-looking condo that didn't quite feel like home yet, he realized he actually felt more comfortable at Penny's house. He still hadn't unloaded most of his boxes, the cabinets were empty, the walls and tabletops, too, whereas at Penny's, everything was warm and tidy and inviting. But then he shook his head. *Don't even go there.* He'd been smart to leave, smart to put his job and his future first. Of course, being so smart had also left him feeling like a jerk, because he'd seen the pain in her eyes and he'd ignored it. Just walked away.

Grabbing a beer from the fridge, he popped the top and let out a sigh. He was an ass. For approaching her in the foyer like that, for letting his desires get the best of him, for running out on her like some kind of coward the moment he'd come to his senses.

It would've been so damn easy to stay, and he wished he was in bed with her right now, holding her afterward, talking, laughing—he hadn't been able to do any of that the first time. He loved Penny's laugh. And he loved the way she scrunched up her nose when something irritated her. Even her feet had been sexy. It was just a shame she hadn't turned out to be the simple girl he'd originally thought.

The way he'd wanted her tonight had nearly ripped him apart inside, and the unfulfilled ache still lingered between his legs. But just like last night, even as much as he regretted the reality of their situation, he'd known leaving was best. Even as that phone call had ruined something close to sheer perfection, it had also saved him.

Just then, he caught sight of the little red light blinking across the room. He was surprised to see he had a phone message, unsure who would be calling him. Unless it was Penny, and he doubted she even had his number. Or Martin, God forbid. He wasn't sure how he'd ever face his boss again, but at least he had a few more days before he had to. A few more days to try to get this whole thing with Penny into the past, where it wouldn't seem quite so overwhelming.

Taking a long swallow of beer, he crossed the ceramic tile and pressed the playback button. "Hello, Ryan, it's your mother." She always did that, always told him who she was, as if he wouldn't be able to tell. "Your father and I wanted to see if you're getting settled, but I guess you're not home. We'll talk to you soon."

According to the clock on the microwave, it was almost ten, so if he called back right now, he'd catch them before they went to bed. Not that he was particularly in the mood to chat with his parents. Oh, he loved them and knew they loved him, too, but he had enough on his mind already without having to hear the latest wonderful news about his older brother, which any conversation with his mom and dad was sure to produce.

Thinking about that old swing in the yard today had briefly reminded Ryan that, once upon a time, he and Dan had been close, but that was ancient history. Just like with his parents, he loved his brother, yet they'd grown apart. They were very different people and their lives had led them down opposite paths. Dan was the smart one, the selfless one, the settled one—the perfect son. He was everything two parents could hope for, and though Ryan didn't think his mom and dad intended for him to feel Dan was their favorite, he still did.

Taking another sip of beer, Ryan let that remind him just how much he didn't want to screw up again. He'd never been a bad kid, but it was hard living up to a brother like Dan. No matter what good things Ryan accomplished, it was the bad that seemed to stand out next to his brother's perfection. He could still hear the disappointment in his father's voice along with his mother's despairing sigh when he'd told them about losing his job at ComData. The worst part was that they hadn't sounded very surprised.

Grabbing the phone before he talked himself out of it, Ryan dialed the same phone number his family had had since he was a little boy.

"Hello?" His father's voice sounded gruff and scratchy, and it reminded Ryan how old they were getting.

"Hey, Dad, it's me."

"Ryan," he said in recognition. "Your mother called you earlier, but you weren't there. Here, I'll put her on."

Good old Dad, never much for small talk.

"Hello, Ryan," his mother said a few seconds later.

"Hey, Mom. Sorry to call so late, but I just got in."

"That's all right; Dan and Carol just left. We were helping them pick out songs for church this Sunday. Did you know Dan is leading the choir now?"

Figures. "No. No, I didn't."

"Well, Miss Higgins has a bad hip and can't stand up that long anymore, so Dan volunteered to take over for her. And just in time, too, because the Summer Songfest is only two weeks away and the choir has to be ready."

Ryan found himself nodding into the phone even though he knew his mother couldn't see him. It was an old habit left over from when he'd lived at home, because he'd grown tired of saying, "Yeah," and "Uh-huh," when listening to constant news of Dan. His parents never seemed to notice his lack of response.

"Well, I won't keep you," Ryan said, "but I just

wanted to let you know things are going fine here. The job is great and I really like the company."

"Are you eating?"

Ryan laughed. Worry over his eating habits was the one way his mother showered concern on him. If he was at home, she was plying him with food, and if he wasn't, she was lecturing him about it. "Not at the moment, Mom. But don't worry, I've got something in the oven right now and I'm keeping myself adequately fed."

"Junk food, I'll bet."

He spent another fleeting thought on Penny's pot roast and said, "Not all the time. Don't worry, I'm fine. And hey—" time to change the subject, he decided "—the condo is great. You guys should think about making a trip down here in the fall."

His mother stayed quiet. Predictably. It had been the same every time he'd invited them to Chicago, too. Finally, she said, "We'll see." Which really meant no. They only wanted to see him when he came home, when he was willing to revisit *their* life.

"Okay, Mom," he said, trying to sound resilient. "I'm kinda tired, though, so I'd better go."

They said their goodbyes and Ryan hung up, feeling as hollow as such conversations usually left him. Oh well, at least the call was out of the way now.

Sniffing the air, Ryan caught a whiff of something hot...burning! Plunking his beer can on the counter, he dashed to the stove and yanked open the oven door.

Damn. Nothing like crunchy pizza rolls.

Fumbling for a pot holder, thankful he'd even remembered to use one the way his night was going, he rescued the pan from the oven and decided the garlic bread didn't look like a total washout, only a little brown around the edges.

He didn't bother hunting for a plate, just took the whole pan to the table, lowering it to a woven place mat, then grabbed his beer and sat down. He'd planned on doing some work on Penny's system tonight, but as he popped the first crisp pizza roll into his mouth, he decided he really was too tired; he was going to go to bed and get some rest.

And he was going to wake up with a new attitude, he vowed. No more messing around, no more taking chances, no more wild women, no more anything that could ruin his life in any way. He might resent his parents, but he still couldn't help wanting, wishing, to make them proud.

None of this was Penny's fault—well, except for the first incident in the limo—but either way, Ryan had to be done with this, done with her. She might be cute and fun and sweet and sexy, but that didn't matter. Starting tomorrow, no more Penny. Well, no more Penny outside of their working relationship, something he didn't have much of a choice in. And to facilitate that, he was going to set a new number one priority—get Penny's computer fixed, so they wouldn't have to meet at her house any longer.

"THE PARTY YOU ARE trying to reach is unavailable. Please leave a message."

Penny sneered at the phone in response as she stood behind the closed door of the pub's office the next morning. But today she had enough wits about her to do as the voice instructed. "Martin, call me as soon as you get this." Then she hung up and exited the office, where it appeared a small mid-morning rush on coffee and Danishes was just dying down. It was raining outside—the only thing to cool the city in a week—and rain always brought in the coffee drinkers.

"Sorry," she said to Patti, who'd handled the whole rush alone. None of the other servers clocked in until eleven, since mornings were usually quiet.

"No biggie," her sister replied, wiping her hands on a towel. Penny joined her behind the bar and as the last customer went out the door, paper bag in hand, Patti lifted her gaze. "So what were you cleaning last night?"

Penny blinked, feeling as if her sister had just flashed a bright light into her eyes. "Nice segue."

Patti snapped her fingers repeatedly. "Come on, come on, answer me, quick. What did you clean?"

"Uh...floors," Penny claimed, wishing she had more experience at lying.

"With a mop or on your hands and knees?"

Recalling having said she was up to her elbows in suds, she smugly replied, "Hands and knees."

Patti reached down to grab one of Penny's wrists and they both looked down at five perfectly manicured nails. "Liar," Patti said.

Penny sighed. She really did hate being dishonest with Patti, but she still couldn't tell her about what had happened in the limo because something about it continued to feel so intimate, so private, so painfully personal.

"Do I have to twist this," Patti asked, still gripping Penny's arm, "or are you gonna spill?"

Penny narrowed her eyes, and decided to tell her sister as much as she could. "You want to know what I was really doing when you called last night? Fine. I was standing in the foyer making out with Ryan in my underwear. Happy now?"

Patti's jaw dropped and Penny took perverse pleasure in having shocked her. "Ryan, the sexy computer guy?"

"That's the one."

Patti sucked in her breath and tightened her grip on Penny's wrist. "Pen, does this mean you're not..."

"Marrying Martin? Correct. I'm not." She glanced at the clock above the bar. "Now I just wish he would call, so I could tell him."

"He doesn't know yet?"

Penny shook her head. "In fact," she sighed, feeling more than a little sheepish, "I may as well tell you. I, uh, didn't exactly have sex with him the other night, either."

"*Exactly?* What does that mean?"

Penny really did want to be as honest as possible, but... "It's complicated," she said, pulling her arm away to straighten a perfectly straight row of glasses and congratulating herself on having said something entirely truthful. "But all that really matters is that we didn't do it."

She feared Patti would be angry or hurt that she'd lied, but when Penny looked back at her sister's eyes, they shone with happiness. "You made the right decision," she said, then grabbed back onto both of Penny's wrists. "And, oh my God, Pen, you and the hot computer babe! How did this happen? Tell me everything. And is it...serious?"

Penny ignored everything else Patti had said except the last part since it stood out the most. She almost wanted to laugh at the very *suggestion* that it could be serious, since it was undoubtedly the most unserious, meaningless relationship she'd ever indulged in, at least from his point of view. But her heart hurt too much to even force any laughter, so she just tried for an easygoing expression. "No. In fact, he sort of dumped me already."

A look of horror reshaped Patti's face. "What happened?"

Penny released a heavy breath, realizing she was sending her sister on a veritable roller-coaster ride of emotion. "Martin is his boss. And Martin wants to marry me. You do the math."

"Oh," Patti said, catching on to the dilemma. "Oh, Pen, I'm so sorry."

Penny shook her head. "It wasn't important. Just a fling."

"You're lying again," her sister said without missing a beat. "You've never had a fling in your life, and besides, I can see it in your eyes. You've always been lousy at hiding your feelings."

Which meant, Penny thought, that Ryan had probably seen it last night, too—her hurt, her sadness. But who cared anyway? Chemistry aside, who needed a guy that held her feelings in such low regard?

"Well, it looks like I've had a fling *now*. But I'm over it," she added, which wasn't entirely true, but no one needed to know that. And when Ryan showed up at her house this afternoon, she was going to fill him in, as well. The new and improved Penny she'd discovered last night after his departure was more than just wild, she was assertive, too, and she wasn't going to put up with this now-I-want-you, now-I-don't stuff. She intended to make her position clear, show him she wouldn't be walked on, and then he'd be sorry he couldn't have her.

Patti took her hands and tried to look cheerful. "How about if Scott and I take you out to dinner tonight?"

Penny could only guess that her firm independence had failed to show on her face just now, since her sister obviously felt sorry for her.

"Thanks, Patti, but I'll pass. I've always hated doing the third wheel thing."

"You wouldn't be a third wheel, I promise. And I want you to get to know him better."

Patti's current boyfriend had popped into the pub for lunch a couple of times, but Penny had never had the chance for more than a hello. "Why? Is *your* thing getting serious?"

Patti hedged a little, but resembled a bashful little girl when she finally smiled. "Kind of. Maybe."

Penny gave her sister a quick hug, accompanied by a reassuring smile. "I'm glad. One of us should have a happy love life."

"Sure I can't talk you into dinner?" Patti asked again.

"Some other night, okay?"

She did want to get better acquainted with Scott—she couldn't remember the last time she'd seen her sister blush over a guy—but the timing was all wrong. Too much remained up in the air. Oh, she certainly didn't expect Ryan to stay at her house late again—in fact, she would make sure to get him out the door by five—but she wanted to be home in case Martin called. She wanted to close this crazy chapter of her life, then move on.

As SHE HAD for the past few days, Penny left the Two Sisters Pub just after the lunch rush, knowing Ryan would arrive around two. Upon getting home, the first thing she did was check her answering machine, but no message, no Martin. The second thing she did was change into a pair of jeans—the rain had persisted and given Penny a slight summer chill. Rather than retucking her Two Sisters T-shirt, which had gotten damp and limp from the rain, she twisted the bottom into a knot, then swept her rain-frizzed hair up on her head into a loose bun.

Next, she pulled up her system notes on the computer. She knew they would review whatever new screens Ryan had created first, but thought she may as well be ready to keep the work rolling. Just as she opened the pertinent file, the doorbell rang.

Taking a deep breath, ready to put all this foolishness with him to an end, she rose and whisked opened the door.

He stood on the front stoop, putting down his umbrella and looking just as handsome as ever. But she was going to ignore that completely. She held open the screen door and let him in out of the rain.

"We have to talk," he said, before even laying down his umbrella or taking off his trench coat.

"I agree." She crossed her arms.

"We can't keep doing what we've been doing. We can't keep...getting close. As in physically."

Penny let out a sigh of annoyance and rolled her eyes. "Yes, I think we keep agreeing on that, too."

But she didn't think he'd even heard her since he rambled right on. "I'm thirty years old and dedicated to settling down and excelling in my career. And I've already been through my swinging single stage, and I just can't go there again, as much as I might like to. Okay?"

"Well," she said, just as directly, "I have news for you, too. I figured something out last night after you left."

"What's that?"

"You were right. I *want* to be wild! I *want* to have fun!

I want to do things I've never done before! And the last thing I need in my life is a man who can't deal with that. That means Martin *and* you."

Ryan's knees nearly gave out. She *wanted* to be wild now? And she wanted to get wild with someone other than *him*? Alarm raced through his body at lightning speed and his stomach twisted in pain as images of her with another man pummeled him. "Who, then? I mean...you're not just gonna go out and—"

"No, of course not!" she snapped, and relief chased the worry from his mind, but he still felt unsteady. "And it's not like I have some particular guy in mind, and it's not even like I'm on the hunt, for heaven's sake, but when I meet the right one, I'll know it. And *he* won't tell me how bad I am for him."

Ryan let out a huge sigh. He felt awful. And sick. He'd thought he had this all figured out, thought he was going to come here, state his case, be completely sturdy and stalwart—even when desire struck—then leave feeling like a new man.

Instead, he felt as if he'd been run over by a truck. The last thing he'd expected was to find out she didn't want him anymore. *And* that she was in the market for somebody else, somebody new, even if she'd claimed afterward that she wasn't.

Aborting his original plan, he ran a hand back through his damp hair, trying to summon the right words, trying to make up for everything he'd done wrong here. "I'm sorry I said that, about you being bad for me. I shouldn't blame you for my issues." He shifted his weight from one foot to the other, realizing that after all they'd been through in the few days they'd known each other, the least he owed her was some honesty. "But the thing is—" he met her gaze and lowered his voice "—I've never said no to myself on much of anything before. So I have to this time or else what kind of man am I? I can't keep screwing up my life for the sake of just doing what I want, doing what feels good at any particular moment." Oh hell, he wasn't saying this right. He needed to get to the heart of the matter, which was her. "But if I could, Penny..."

Her eyes changed then, looking as though they belonged to someone much more gentle than the girl who'd just announced her sexual independence. "Yes?"

"Well, let's just say I'd give anything to help you explore this side of yourself, because it's a damn appealing side."

She swallowed visibly, appeared nervous. Dropped her gaze, but raised it once more. "Really?"

He lowered his eyes, too, seeing for the first time that her feet were bare again, peeking from the bottom of her blue jeans. He nodded, and his groin began to tighten. Just over her feet? he wondered, incredulous. No, over all of her, every beautiful ounce of her. From her sweet, trusting eyes to the way her T-shirt hugged her breasts to the pale pink polish on her toenails. Part of him wished he hadn't said so much, been so honest, but he'd had to. He couldn't be so cold without at least letting her know why.

And it was in that moment of silence that Ryan finally understood the whole problem here.

When she'd seduced him in the limousine, he'd had no choice but to see her as some strong, bold, take-charge woman who wanted nothing more from him than a good time. Yet every minute they'd spent together since then had altered his thinking. She *was* that strong, bold woman; he knew it, he'd lived it. But she was also soft and vulnerable, the sort of woman who needed more than just the physical act of sex. And that part of her got to him. Down deep.

Maybe he'd almost begun to believe her when she insisted she wasn't wild, when she said the limo incident had been an aberration. But now she was changing her story again, telling him just the opposite, and he suddenly understood—she couldn't be labeled. It wasn't that simple, and it complicated everything within him even further.

And yet, still more important was the fact that what he'd just said was so true: No matter who she was— June Cleaver or the sexy siren from the limo—he couldn't have her. Just couldn't.

"Have you talked to Martin yet?" he asked, just to say something.

"No. I called his hotel, but he hasn't called me back." She shifted her weight, the move jostling her breasts ever so slightly, and before he could stop himself, he wondered what kind of bra she wore under that T-shirt today.

"I'm sure he'll call soon."

"I hope so. I really want this settled. And this thing with *you* settled, too." Her resentful gaze shot through him. *You're not the guy for me*, she was saying again. *You're not the guy who'll give me what I need.*

Ah, damn, he wanted to give it to her. And it seemed pure insanity that he'd turn down the offer of this beautiful woman to help her explore her sexuality, but she was right; the sooner the whole fiasco was settled, the better off they'd both be.

"I'm, uh, not gonna stay and work with you today," he said. "Sorry I didn't let you know sooner, but I didn't get much done this morning, so I don't have anything new to show you. I just came by to look at your floppy drive like I promised."

He walked past her, not bothering to shed his raincoat since this would only take a minute. She followed, but he didn't look at her, just dropped to his knees upon reaching the desk, then took out the miniature tool kit he'd brought in his briefcase.

Removing the computer's cover, he wrangled and toyed with the wedged diskette until it popped free. But one look into the empty drive told him it was shot. "It's broken," he announced.

"I knew that."

"I mean, I got the diskette out, but if you put another one in, it'll stick again." Grabbing a notepad to write down the specifics about her computer, he added, "I'll order a new floppy drive for you tomorrow, and see if I can locate a new modem, too."

She seemed taken aback by the offer. "You don't have to do that."

He still didn't look at her as he snapped the cover back into place and got to his feet. "I don't mind. Besides, I'm guessing most of your computer help has come from Martin lately, and you never know, after he hears that you're not gonna marry him, it might *never* get fixed."

She sighed. "You make a good point. Thanks…for the help."

He shook his head, at a loss for what else to say. But in his gut, he felt how easy it would still be to kiss her, and he smelled her damn shampoo again, even from a few feet away.

"I'd better go."

"Yes," she murmured. "Yes, you should."

Ryan returned his tools to his briefcase and snapped

it shut, then picked up his umbrella. After pausing only long enough for one brief look into her pretty eyes, he headed for the door, but as he lowered his hand to the knob, he stopped and peered over his shoulder. "Penny, before I leave, I just have to know something."

"What's that?"

"The scent of your shampoo. What is it?"

"Uh...mango," she said, clearly bewildered. "Why?"

"No reason." He shook his head. "I just like it." Then he walked out into the rain.

Reaching the brick path below her porch, he put up his umbrella and trudged through the heavy drizzle toward the sidewalk that lined the quaint residential street. *Mango.* Sounded exotic. Erotic. Kind of...wild. Just like the girl he was leaving behind.

He was really doing that, leaving her behind—Penny the Sandwich Girl, Penny the limousine seductress, Penny of the lavender bra. Pretty Penny.

Just put one foot in front of the other. You can do it.

But at the very thought of feet, hers came to mind. Why did he have to find them so sexy? Of course, he'd gotten a little peek at her belly button beneath her knotted shirt, too. Equally sexy, and not as weird for him to be aroused by. It seemed impossible that he'd seen so much more of her just last night and managed to walk out the door, yet today these little flashes of skin were making him nuts.

Just keep moving, he told himself. *You made it out last night, and you've made it out today, too. Piece of cake. Nothin' to it.*

Though a disturbing image assaulted him as he trod up the sidewalk. It was Penny, back in the limo, but this time the lights were on. She was shedding her clothes, piece by delectable piece, before lowering herself into *another man's* lap, straddling him as she'd straddled Ryan. She gazed into the new guy's eyes, ran her hands through his hair, and whispered in his ear. *I want to be wild.*

Ryan swallowed, all too aware of the raging jealousy pulsing through his body. Not to mention the nagging bulge that had grown beneath his pants. This woman was killing him. It wasn't even her fault, but she was driving him mad. "Damn it," he muttered, stopping. He turned and looked back down the street, realizing he'd passed his car, probably right around the time Penny had wiggled from her panties in his mind. "Damn it, damn it, damn it."

He started back toward the sedan, watching as it grew nearer through the rain, until he was almost there. The only problem now was that he wanted her more than he wanted to breathe. And he kept right on walking.

A moment later, he stood on her porch, one finger pressing down the doorbell, blood pumping through his veins like liquid heat.

Penny pulled open the door and stared at him through the screen.

"I'm back," he said.

"Why?"

"I'm weak?"

Her eyes, a dark, misty shade of blue that somehow matched the rain, widened with that moment of absorbing the unexpected.

Then, slowly, they turned sexy and oh-so-inviting as she bit her lip and reached for the door handle. "Come in."

6

As Ryan stepped in from the chilling rain, the heat in Penny's gaze hit him like a sledgehammer. Everything they'd done in the limo had been heaven on earth, but he hadn't been able to see her beautiful eyes then. The unspoken desire that shone in them now changed everything. And he was about to trade his career for the look in those eyes, but he didn't have an ounce of regret.

His briefcase thudded to the floor and his umbrella followed. Without a word, he stepped forward to kiss her. Cupping her cheeks, his hands were gentle, but his kiss was not. He felt like a man who'd just crossed a desert and she was his first drink of water.

When the kiss ended, she looked up at him, her breathing labored. "You're not holding anything back."

"What?" he murmured.

Her lips trembled. "That night in the limo, I could tell you were holding back. Even though you kissed me senseless, I knew there was more of you I wasn't quite getting."

"I was caught off guard then. Hell, I'm always caught off guard with you."

She curled her fingers into tight fists, the fabric of his shirt crushed within. "Don't hold anything back *now*, Ryan."

Her words swept through him like wildfire. "Don't

worry, honey. I couldn't if I tried." And he meant it; he hadn't come back here to do anything halfway.

He lowered his mouth to hers again as she pushed the wet raincoat along with his suit jacket from his shoulders. The clothing fell to the floor in a heap behind him and she started working at his tie. His breath came heavy as his hands roamed up from her hips to graze her breasts, his fingertips playing across the hardened peaks beneath her shirt to make her moan.

His aching erection pressed against the juncture of her thighs as he leaned her against the wall. She moved into him, a slight, teasing grind at first, then more urgent, until he lost himself in the hot friction. He kissed her with all the pent-up passion he'd harbored these past few agonizing days—it felt more like weeks, months—and his only thought was drinking in more of her, somehow taking her into his soul.

When he finally pulled back from the kiss, their hips still locked in rough need, Ryan witnessed such wrenching passion in her eyes that it shot straight to his heart, and he suddenly understood the truth. *This really mattered to her.*

He'd known that before, known she was a woman who didn't take sex lightly, but he'd obviously underestimated her feelings. Yes, she was eager and anxious to explore her sexuality, but as he fell captive to the raw emotion on her face, he knew more than ever that her actions also had to do with her heart.

And while that might normally have had him pulling back, thinking twice, he couldn't pull away from Penny this time. He didn't have the power; her wringing need drew him like a magnet. And maybe that meant it mattered to him, too, but right now, he wasn't capable of thinking beyond this moment, and he wasn't even sure he *wanted* to look any deeper at his own response to the woman in his arms.

Unknotting her T-shirt, he pulled it off over her head to reveal a seductive powder-blue bra that matched her eyes. Her breasts swelled from the hugging fabric, her rosy nipples visible through the lacy edge. "You're so sexy," he murmured.

Nuzzling her, he dropped a few soft, lingering kisses on her neck, shoulder, and was just about to use his teeth to ease down one bra strap when suddenly she clung tight to him. "Ryan, don't leave me this time."

The whispered words stunned him at first, but then his heart broke for every time he'd left her, even in the limo. He wished now he'd stayed. "I won't. I promise," he answered, his voice strained, his chest tightening at his own words. This was surrender, total and complete.

Penny hated what she'd just said, how she'd let her resolve be diminished, but when he'd come back to her door, the thrill that'd rushed through her had been paralyzing, and now his touches had weakened her. She'd told him the truth—she didn't want a guy who didn't want the same things she did—but saying it and sticking to it were two different things. What she felt with Ryan right now went beyond any normal sort of passion. Just as she'd feared last night, she cared for him. And she also feared she'd just let him see her true feelings.

Yet still he held her, had not pulled away.

More than that, he kissed her, slower now, his lips playing gently over hers as his hands skimmed down her back and bottom.

When Penny finally unbuttoned his shirt and shoved it from his shoulders, one glimpse of his chest undid her. She'd felt its broad, smooth planes beneath her hands in the limo, had even seen it briefly after the light had come on, but now everything was different—every touch, every word, every glance went deeper.

"You're so beautiful," Ryan whispered, "you make me ache."

The compliment spread through her. "Don't worry. I think I can relieve that ache."

As he reached for the button on her jeans, Penny pulled in her breath, her entire body tingling beneath the lust in his gaze. She couldn't quite believe she'd just said that, and she couldn't quite believe that this was her, opening up completely, abandoning herself to such brazen desire. Then a knock came on the door.

She flinched and Ryan's fingers stilled. They exchanged startled looks and her heartbeat kicked up another notch. This was just like the phone call last night, which had ruined everything. "I won't answer it," she whispered. "They'll go away."

As if on cue, though, the knock sounded again, this time accompanied by a voice. "Come on, Pen, I know you're home."

Penny gasped. "Oh no, it's Patti. And she does know I'm home. My car's outside and I'm supposed to be here...*working* with you."

Ryan let out a frustrated sigh.

"I'll get rid of her," Penny said.

"Penny?" Her sister yelled through the door, knocking again.

"Hurry," Ryan whispered, and the urgency in his voice shot straight to the juncture of Penny's thighs.

"Coming!" she called, and she was just about to break free of Ryan's embrace and grab her shirt when the door burst open and Patti stepped in, Scott behind her.

We'd like to send you **2 FREE** books and a surprise gift to introduce you to Harlequin Temptation®. Accept our special offer today and

Indulge in a Harlequin Moment!

HOW TO QUALIFY:

1. With a coin, carefully scratch off the silver area on the card at right to see what we have for you—**2 FREE BOOKS** and a **FREE GIFT**—**ALL YOURS! ALL FREE!**

2. Send back the card and you'll receive two brand-new Harlequin Temptation® books. These books have a cover price of $3.99 each in the U.S. and $4.50 each in Canada, but they are yours to keep absolutely free!

3. There's no catch. You're under no obligation to buy anything. We charge nothing— ZERO—for your first shipment and you don't have to make any minimum number of purchases—not even one!

4. The fact is, thousands of readers enjoy receiving books by mail from the Harlequin Reader Service®. They enjoy the convenience of home delivery... they like getting the best new novels at discount prices, BEFORE they're available in stores...and they love their *Heart to Heart* subscriber newsletter featuring author news, horoscopes, recipes, book reviews and much more!

5. We hope that after receiving your free books you'll want to remain a subscriber. But the choice is yours—to continue or cancel, any time at all. So why not take us up on our invitation with no risk of any kind. You'll be glad you did!

SPECIAL FREE GIFT!

We can't tell you what it is...but we're sure you'll like it! A FREE gift just for giving the Harlequin Reader Service® a try!

Visit us online at
www.eHarlequin.com

The **2 FREE BOOKS** we send you will be selected from **HARLEQUIN TEMPTATION**®, the series that brings you sexy, sizzling and seductive stories.

Books received may vary.

Scratch off the silver area to see what the Harlequin Reader Service has for you.

2 FREE BOOKS and a FREE GIFT!

HARLEQUIN®
Makes any time special™

YES! I have scratched off the silver area above. Please send me the **2 FREE** books and gift for which I qualify. I understand I am under no obligation to purchase any books, as explained on the back and on the opposite page.

342 HDL DH4W   142 HDL DH4V

FIRST NAME   LAST NAME

ADDRESS

APT.#   CITY

STATE/PROV.   ZIP/POSTAL CODE

Offer limited to one per household and not valid to current Harlequin Temptation® subscribers. All orders subject to approval.

"Scott got off work early and we decided to take in a, uh, matinee." Her smile froze on her face as Scott's eyes widened until they looked as if they might pop from his head.

Penny and Ryan stood equally frozen and Penny wanted to die. Scott's gaze was glued to her and despite the fact he'd probably seen women wearing frilly bras before, he'd never seen *her* in one. She could barely speak. "I *said* I was coming," she managed to choke out to her sister.

Patti's smile had faded to the same horror-filled expression the rest of them wore. "Oops. I thought you said 'Come in.'" Then she spoke quickly, wringing her hands. "We just wanted to see if you'd changed your mind about meeting us for dinner later, but I'm guessing for sure now you haven't."

This time, Ryan answered for her. "Yeah, I think she'll be busy."

"Sorry," Patti said, backing out the door, stumbling into Scott, who now studied his shoes as he repeatedly ran his hands back through his blond hair. "Bye."

As the door closed, shutting out the intrusion and the sound of the lightly falling rain, Penny peered up at Ryan, still in his loose embrace.

"Now returning from the Twilight Zone," he said, looking nearly as dumbfounded as she felt.

"I can't believe that just happened," she said, her face hot from embarrassment. "I can't believe my sister's boyfriend just saw me half-undressed!"

And I can't believe this had to happen now, right when we were about to make wild, passionate love. Penny's heart sank as the expression on Ryan's face immediately overrode her worry about Scott. They'd been here before, after all, and she could guess what was coming. He would change his mind, he'd remember Martin and his job, and all the glorious passion they'd just been sharing would fall apart.

But Ryan simply pushed back a loose strand of her hair. "Oh, come on now," he murmured, "you're not really *half*-undressed." He leaned near, their faces lingering close for a slow, sexy moment before he lowered his mouth to hers. She let the kiss melt down through her, finally understanding that she'd been wrong and this *wasn't* ending. He still wanted her.

"To be half-undressed," Ryan said, "this would have to be gone." He ran one finger down the strap of her bra. "Or, at the very least, these would have to come off." His touch returned to the front of her blue jeans and a wave of heat rushed through her body. As he lowered the zipper, she quivered at the sensations just beneath. He slid his hands inside, over her hips, pushing down the denim and giving a little growl as she wriggled free to reveal a skimpy swath of blue lace underneath.

"Of course," he whispered, "we're not gonna stop at just the halfway point." He reached for her again, this time raining soft kisses on the exposed skin above her bra. Lowering the blue straps until her breasts spilled free, he took one stiffened peak into his mouth, and she braced herself against the wall for support as his ministrations echoed through her. Oh, how she wanted this man, and how she trusted him so much, already. She'd never let a man get this close to her so quickly, but she found herself wanting to know all his secrets, his entire past, his dreams for the future; she wanted to be a *part* of that future.

When he straightened, he cupped her face in his

hands. "Tell me about your fantasies, Penny. Let me make them come true."

She bit her lip, nervous. Ryan was so sexy, and so comfortable and confident, that for a moment it frightened her. But a few minutes ago, she reminded herself, you actually told him you could relieve his ache, so she forced her nervousness aside. She wanted to be what she'd claimed she was—she wanted to be wild for him.

Trying to summon a reply, her thoughts flashed on the previous evening. "Last night after you left, I took a bath, and even though I was mad at you, I wished you were there. I..." Could she really say this part? "I imagined things...things you'd do to me in the tub."

Without prelude, he scooped her up in his arms, and carried her to the bathroom.

Soon they settled into frothy bubbles, their legs mingling beneath the water, but Penny panicked a little, fearing this sort of intimacy was too much, too fast, despite how eager she felt. It had been one thing to make love in the limo, in the dark, when she'd thought he was someone she knew, but this suddenly seemed more difficult, as if it were the *real* first time.

Ryan leaned back in the tub and gave her a slow, sultry smile. "So, last night, when you were thinking about us like this, what did I do to you?"

Her chest fluttered. Maybe it *was* too much, too fast, but it was also too tempting to resist. Her voice came breathy. "You...used the sponge."

Ryan's expression became serious as he reached for the seashell-shaped sponge, along with her Sunny Peach body wash, resting on the shelf behind the tub. When he met her eyes in silent command, she emerged from the bubbles, rising to her knees between his legs, and all her fear vanished, chased away by anticipation.

As he swiped the sponge slowly across her stomach, arms, breasts, Penny fell victim to the pleasure taking control of her body. When he drew it up the center of her in one long, luxurious stroke, she felt it everywhere, and something clenched tight deep in her womb.

"How am I doing?" he asked softly. "Anything like your fantasy?"

"Better."

"Tell me what happened next."

She lowered herself over his hips until she met his incredible hardness beneath the bubbles. "Sex."

Releasing a groan, Ryan slid his wet hands to her soapy bottom to guide her, and she sank easily onto him, although the sensation nearly took her breath. She remembered what this felt like the first night, yet it seemed startlingly new. Instinct made her move on him in slow circles and she peered into his eyes the entire time, never looking away. She finally had that glorious connection between their eyes as their bodies connected below. Their gazes stayed locked until she shattered into a bliss that splashed water from the tub and left them both groaning with pleasure.

They never spoke after that, but Ryan kissed her, slow and thorough, before lifting her from the tub. Grabbing a towel to wrap around her, he carried her down the hall to her bed. Mauve miniblinds kept the room warm and dim, the rain outside creating even more shadows. He opened her peach towel and parted her thighs, kneeling in between.

"My fantasy now," he whispered, and bent to rake his tongue across her most sensitive spot, kissing and licking until Penny was biting her lip, lost to the tumult of sensation. She gripped the brass railings over her head until she was lifting herself against his mouth, moaning with each pulse of heat that swept through her. When she came this time, it was harder, fiercer, making her clench her teeth and whimper until there were only sighs, hers and his, as he slid up beside her on the bed.

Gazing into his eyes, Penny realized how far gone she was. Frightening words echoed through her mind. *I love you.* She wanted to say them, but they couldn't be true, not this soon, not this quickly. Yet it didn't diminish the power of the emotion in her heart when she whispered, "Make love to me some more."

Ryan rolled himself on top of her without delay, entering her with ease. She peered up at him playfully and said, "This is the first time we've done it in a bed."

He brushed his fingertips through her hair and gave her a gentle smile. "Probably not exactly the kind of thing you fantasize about, huh?"

Beneath him, Penny didn't answer, didn't tell him the truth that reverberated inside her.

Yes. It is.

WHEN PENNY AWOKE with Ryan's arm looped around her waist, they lay atop her comforter, the towel bunched beneath them. She turned to watch him sleeping, his head sharing a pillow with hers. Her heart nearly burst just watching him breathe, studying his dark eyelashes, noticing the lock of hair that fell over his forehead. Making love to him—for that's truly what it had been, making love—had been the most thrilling, fulfilling experience Penny could ever remember.

Which was kind of scary considering their circumstances, and especially since she could barely fathom how daring she'd been, but she didn't have time to deal with the worries as Ryan stretched and opened his eyes.

"Hi," she said.

He smiled. "Hi."

She swallowed, nervous. This was the aftermath, the moment when she'd find out if he regretted what they'd done. "How...are you?"

"Good," he said, then his grin turned rakish. "Satisfied." He pulled her a little closer. "And you?"

"The same."

He kissed her forehead. "I like helping you live out your fantasies, Penny."

Something inside her tingled, and she didn't know if it was emotional or sexual, or both. "Really?"

"Oh yeah," he growled, then leaned down to nip playfully at the pebbled tip of her breast.

She let out a laugh as relief skittered through her. She'd been so afraid he'd regret it. "Hungry, are you?" she teased him.

His expression turned sheepish. "Actually, I've been thinking about pot roast sandwiches, among other things, since I left here last night."

"Why don't I go whip a couple up and bring them back? It'll only take a minute."

"Hmm," he said, "dinner in bed. We could start a new trend."

Even though she'd offered, Penny hated pulling away from him, hated ending this perfect moment. But she had to be mature here; she knew this was only a fling, knew that's all it could be. So she couldn't act clingy and emotional...well, not any more than she already had.

Grabbing a short, silky kimono from a hook on her closet door, she headed for the kitchen and returned five minutes later carrying a tray laden with hot pot roast sandwiches, potato chips and two glasses of milk.

"I made an assumption about the milk," she told him, lowering the tray to the bed.

"A girl after my own heart," he said with a smile. "Nothing goes better with home-cooking."

As they ate, they talked about her business and more about her family, about how he'd gotten into software design back in college, and about pets they'd once owned and their favorite TV shows growing up. Penny savored each nugget of information, every little insight into his soul. But she also worried that this would be a onetime thing, that they might never share such good, easy, gratifying communication again.

This must be what it's like, she thought, what people who have flings talk about after sex. Only then they went home afterward and it didn't matter anymore. They thought of it as something pleasant, something fun, but it was just one incident, one experience, it wasn't something that ebbed its way into their souls as Penny could feel this discussion doing right now.

"I, uh, hope your sister wasn't in Martin's corner," Ryan said then.

She shook her head, understanding the implications. "No, she's thrilled I'm not marrying him. In fact, I even told her about us—you and me—so walking in on us probably wasn't *quite* the shock it seemed."

"You told her about us?"

Oh, why had she said that? "Well, not about the limo incident. Just that we were having a…" What were they having again? "A…thing. A fling." Yes, that was it.

Worry glimmered in his eyes. "She wouldn't tell—"

"Martin? Of course not. She understands the problem." And for the first time since Patti had left and Ryan had started taking off Penny's clothes again, she wondered if he still had issues. "Dare I ask about that problem? I mean, it's still there."

"To be honest," he said with a sigh, "I'm just not thinking about it right now."

Maybe she was crazy for even bringing this up, being this honest, but she needed to know what he would say. "I was afraid after Patti showed up...that you'd change your mind again and leave."

"Well, *I'm* afraid," he replied, "that I probably couldn't have stopped if Martin himself had walked in."

The admission made Penny smile, but she tried not to think about the full extent of why, or about the emotions bubbling just beneath the surface of her calm exterior.

When the food was gone, Ryan said, "That was great. Really hit the spot." He dropped his eyes briefly before raising them back to hers. "But I'd...better get going. Got a lot of work to do, you know."

"Oh," she said. "Yeah. Of course." She'd been hoping against his leaving, but had been waiting for it just the same.

Together, they rose from the bed and returned to the bathroom, gathering various clothes from the tiled floor. After stepping into his boxer briefs, he grabbed another towel to wipe up the water they'd splashed over the side—luckily, his suit pants had landed far enough away that only the cuffs got wet. He raised his eyebrows and joked with Penny. "I wonder what your neighbors would've thought if I'd gone jogging out to my car in my underwear."

"I guess they'd have been onto me."

"Onto you?"

She hesitantly lifted her gaze, even as the warmth of

a blush climbed her cheeks. "They'd realize I've... changed."

His easy smile reassured her that those changes were okay.

After he was dressed and she stood with him in the foyer, he lifted her hand to his mouth and softly kissed it. "See you tomorrow," he said with a smile. "We'll get back on track with our work then, keep moving forward."

She nodded, secretly thinking, Who cares about the stupid system? But she knew all too well, his job was important to him. "Sounds good."

"And Penny," he said, "me and you, in the tub, and the bed..."

Was he trying to tell her it couldn't happen again? "Yes?"

His voice went lower. "It was *phenomenal*. I'm glad I came back."

He gave her a last smile, lowered a kiss to her forehead, then turned to go, his coat draped over one arm, his briefcase dangling from his other hand. She stood at the screen, watching him walk toward his car. The rain had ended and the streets and sidewalk were already drying.

After closing the door, Penny made her way to the couch, where she plopped down and grabbed a pillow, hugging it in front of her. Joy and sorrow feuded inside her. Letting the joy win for a moment, she leaned her head back, reveling in the memories, in the realized fantasy that had been far more wonderful than anything she'd imagined, and in her true and utter abandon. Even though that part hadn't come quite as easy as she'd thought it would. Looking back, she thought, *What on earth was I doing, moaning and groaning and writhing in his arms?* It had felt so foreign to her, as though someone had taken over her body. But she didn't regret one second of it, either.

Yet, she wondered, biting her lip, did it really count as being wild if she thought she was falling in love? Maybe it wasn't wildness at all. Maybe it was just the beginning of something deeper.

She shook her head in disbelief. Here she was, still trying to turn down one man's proposal, and she thought she might already be starting to fall in love with another.

Well, that part wouldn't matter in the end anyway, since she knew this was just casual sex to Ryan; it *couldn't* be any more than that, at least not as long as he remained at Schuster Systems.

The worst part was she had no idea how things would be between them tomorrow, and no way of knowing if they'd ever make love again.

7

"THE PARTY YOU ARE trying to reach is unavailable. Please leave a message."

Penny hung up the phone in the pub's office with a heavy sigh. Parts of her life were starting to play like a broken record. Which made her all the more thankful Ryan hadn't left before making love to her last night—that was one pattern she'd been especially anxious to alter. She still got tingly inside every time she thought about it, about him.

And as things with Ryan deepened, she burned with the need to talk to Martin, to get this proposal business cleared up. She glanced at her watch. 8:57 a.m. Almost six in Vegas. She'd been certain if she called him this early in the morning, he'd be there.

Picking the phone back up, Penny redialed the Flamingo Hilton's number, which she now knew by heart. This time, however, instead of requesting his room, she asked the operator if she could have a message delivered personally to Mr. Schuster. "What's the message, ma'am?"

Simple. "Call Penny."

She couldn't believe it was Thursday, a week since she'd talked to him. But, she reasoned, Martin always put the company first, so if there was some important early-morning computer seminar, he'd be there. Or maybe he'd just left to meet with potential clients over breakfast. Whatever the case, she could almost imagine his words when he finally got in touch with her. "Penny, I apologize for not calling, but I got so wrapped up in the conference that time got away from me." Then he'd drift off onto a tangent about the marvelous networking opportunities or the new technologies.

"Hello, are you in there?" A brisk knock came on the office door as Patti's voice cut into her thoughts.

Penny swung the door open. "Hi," she said, but knew she sounded dejected.

"What's wrong? And why are you hiding in the office?"

"I was trying to get in touch with Martin, but no luck."

Patti glanced at the phone on the desk, then back at Penny, then broke into a let's-tell-secrets smile. "Well, Martin's not the guy I want to hear about anyway. Tell me everything."

Penny wished she were more annoyed at her sister's nosiness, but it was fun to be the one doing something exciting for a change. She felt as if it put her and Patti on equal ground. Nonetheless, she played aloof, tossing out, "Nothing to tell," as she sauntered past into the pub.

"*Nothing to tell*," Patti mimicked, grabbing her wrist to spin her around. "Well, you can at least tell me where you got that bra. I thought poor Scott would have a heart attack."

Heat filled Penny's cheeks. "Me, too. I have no idea how I'll ever face the guy again. But I'm betting that's the last time you'll come barging into my house like that, huh?"

They both burst into laughter then, even though

Penny's was slightly nervous. Patti's eyes still danced with mirth after they'd quieted. "Come on, Pen. At least tell me if he was good or not."

Penny cast a slow, wicked grin. "Well, he was…just as good as he looks like he'd be."

"Ooh, sounds fun." Patti took on a rather lascivious expression herself before casting a suspicious look. "So what's the deal with you anyway? Something's suddenly very different."

Her sister's powers of perception were truly amazing, but at least Penny still held her limousine encounter secret. It remained the one thing she was determined not to share. "What do you mean?"

"Oh, I don't have a word for it exactly, but…wow, Pen, having sex with a guy you hardly know? That's not like you. And in your foyer, too!"

"We didn't do it in the foyer," Penny cut in, but she had to laugh at her own defensiveness as she added, "It was in the bathtub."

Patti joined in the giggling. "See what I mean? It's like you're a new woman."

"I think I am," Penny confessed. "I've stumbled across a side of myself I never knew before." *Even if it's a side I'm still struggling to get comfortable with.* "A side that'll let me cut loose a little, let me have a full-blown fling for once in my life."

"You lie," Patti accused, her tone shifting.

"What?"

"You keep using that word, *fling,* but new woman or not, I don't believe for a minute that's all this is. You as much as admitted that to me yesterday."

Penny sighed, but stood strong. "Be that as it may, a fling is all it can be, and I'm prepared to deal with that." *I think.*

"Oh, I get it," Patti replied. "You're really digging him, but he's still got this job hang-up going on."

"It's not a hang-up. Martin would probably fire Ryan if he found out. At the very least, it would strain their relationship."

"Maybe he could get a new job," Patti suggested.

"Yeah, he could quit a job he relocated for, so he can date a girl he barely knows. That makes a lot of sense."

"He had sex with you."

Twice, in fact, although Patti didn't know that. "It's the twenty-first century. It happens. I don't think he feels obligated to me just because I invited him into my bathtub."

Penny hated the look that formed on Patti's face. She could see the pity and concern, not to mention the fear that Penny would get her heart broken.

"Don't worry," Penny insisted, "I can handle this." Besides, she had no other choice. She'd let herself go wild with him, and she hadn't asked for promises. "For all I know, it won't even happen again. And if so...I'll live." *Even if I'm miserable for a while.*

When the phone rang, Penny flinched, thinking it was Martin, and raced to snatch up the receiver. "Two Sisters Pub. This is Penny."

"Hi Penny, it's Grace."

She suppressed a groan—still no Martin. "Hi, Grace. What's up?"

"I want to place a breakfast order."

"Breakfast, huh?" She tried to sound lighthearted. "That's different." Schuster Systems ordered five to ten lunches from them every day, but never breakfast.

"I know," Grace laughed, "but Eve, Ryan and I were standing here saying how hungry we are, and we decided some Danishes sounded good. We want two apple, two cheese and one cherry."

Penny scribbled the order, but was stuck on hearing Ryan's name, on envisioning him standing at Grace's desk this very second, listening to their phone call. "Got it. Anything else?"

"No, that's it. I'll be down in five to get them."

"I can bring them up," Penny offered.

"Are you sure?"

"I'm not busy, so why not?"

After she got off the phone, she packed the order and told Patti where she was headed. Patti simply shook her head. "Fling, my butt."

"I'm not going up there just to see *him*. I'm going...to be nice." And that was partially true. She and Grace were casual friends and she knew Grace was busy this time of day, answering phones and dealing with early-morning office duties. In fact, that's how the daily sandwich delivery ritual had originally begun. Grace had been unable to leave the phones for several days in a row at lunchtime, and Penny had offered to start bringing them up.

When she stepped off the elevator a few minutes later at Schuster Systems, everything felt normal. The lobby's chrome trim shone beneath recessed lighting and fresh flower arrangements adorned the tables in the small waiting area. Grace resided behind her circular desk, her hair swept back in its usual bun, and she looked buried in mail-sorting. Penny approached with a smile. "Two apple, two cheese, one cherry," she said, handing over the white bag.

Grace pushed up her tiny glasses. "That was quick."

Penny shrugged. "Five Danishes are easier than five sandwiches."

Just then, Ryan passed through the rear of the lobby behind Grace's desk, a handful of diskettes clutched in his fist. He glanced up, saw Penny, then stopped short. "Uh, hi."

Suddenly nothing felt very normal anymore. Her heart nearly stopped at the sight of his smile on this official "morning after," and she almost smiled back, but then remembered that Grace was sitting right there. "Hi," she said, trying to sound completely casual. "I...brought your Danish."

He seemed to catch on then, his eyes flashing just a hint of alarm. "Great. Thanks."

"I'll bring it back in a minute," Grace told him over her shoulder.

"Thanks," he said again, then gave Penny a quick wink before heading on his way.

"So," Grace said when he was gone, "I bet you're looking forward to Martin's return in a few days."

Penny winced inside, and drew her gaze down to Grace's friendly eyes. "Uh, yeah." *For more reasons than you know.* Then she tilted her head, and took the opportunity to ask the question that had been plaguing her. "Grace, have you heard from Martin since he's been away?"

Grace shook her head. "No, but that's not uncommon. He's such a workaholic, he tends to get so mired in whatever he's doing that he forgets to check in. And he trusts me to keep things moving smoothly while he's away." A hint of pride echoed in her voice.

"Then you don't think it's a little weird that I haven't heard from him, either?"

"Not really. He's probably backing off, trying to give you some space, time to think."

Penny knew Martin had told Grace about his proposal before he'd left. Grace had been with him since Schuster Systems' inception and he tended to share certain personal issues with her as a matter of course.

"That would make sense," Penny said, "except that I've left messages at his hotel."

Grace gave her an encouraging look. "I wouldn't worry, Penny. It's like I said. He's probably completely immersed in conference activities and hasn't even checked his messages. Those events can be really hectic and tiring."

Penny nodded, reassured if not consoled. "Yeah, that's what I was thinking."

"But I'm sure you're on his mind every second." Grace smiled. "I'm sure he's hoping to slip a ring on your finger as soon as he gets back."

That's the part that's eating me alive, she thought. "Thanks, Grace," was all she said.

RYAN FELT GREAT as he moved up Penny's front walk. He *shouldn't* feel great, he knew that. He should feel awful. And it wasn't that he'd quit worrying about Martin and his job, but yesterday with Penny had been incredible! A dart of pleasure arced through him just remembering.

When Ryan looked back on his life, he couldn't remember ever knowing anyone like Penny. He'd dated mostly sophisticated girls, or at least girls who *thought* they were sophisticated—cheerleaders in high school, sorority girls in college, and since then, executive-type women. But something in those relationships had always lacked... What was the word he was searching for? Heart? Substance?

He'd probably talked more with Penny in the short time he'd known her than he ever had with any other woman. It had happened again after they'd made love yesterday. They'd just talked. About everything and nothing. It had been nice. So nice that leaving hadn't come as easy as he would have liked, but he'd done it anyway because it had seemed the prudent thing to do. If he could call anything about yesterday afternoon prudent.

So for now, he had no answers; he just had to go with the flow. The good news was that after he'd gone yesterday, he'd gotten a tremendous amount of work done on her system. Relieving his sexual frustrations with her must have been good for him on more than one level.

When Penny opened the door, she wore brief denim shorts that hugged her slender hips and a bright-red tank top that conformed to her curves, as well. Her sandy-blond hair cascaded over her shoulders. "Hi," she said.

The very sight of her left him speechless. After all, this morning at the office she'd been wearing her Two Sisters T-shirt and baseball cap, which was cute, of course, but now she looked plain sexy. "Uh, hi," he finally sputtered, then realized he was staring. "Sorry. But you look good."

She gave him a bashful smile. "Thanks."

Ah yes, the simpler Penny. But he knew what lay underneath that innocent veneer, and the mere knowledge drove him crazy. He moved closer and slid his arms around her waist, then lowered a kiss to her lips that heated his blood. As she lifted her hands to his chest, he whispered in her ear, "So tell me, what kind of bra are you wearing today?"

He drew back in time to see a coquettish look form in

her eyes. "Wouldn't you like to know." Mmm, the vixen Penny had arrived.

Lifting a hand to her shoulder, Ryan eased his fingers beneath her tank top to reveal an equally red strap. His heart stopped. "Nice. Can I see the rest?"

"Now?" She looked amused.

He let his eyes fall briefly shut and let out a sigh. "You're right. We have to work, don't we?"

"Not that I don't find you tempting," she said, biting her lip in that provocative way he loved, "but working would probably be a good idea, since we didn't yesterday."

To his surprise, Ryan found holding back easier now, likely because he knew there would be more, and because he no longer had to pretend nothing was going on between them. In one sense, he knew falling into this relationship was insane, but he really had surrendered to her yesterday in a way he couldn't ignore. When Martin came home— Well, they'd deal with that then. But for now, things felt too good to worry about the future.

"My computer was finally delivered to the office today," he said, taking a seat at her desk. "While the wholesale guy was there, I ordered your floppy drive and modem."

"Thank you," she replied, walking over to place one hand to his cheek.

He grinned uncertainly. "It's only a couple of computer parts."

"No, that's not what I mean. Thank you for that, too. But what I'm really thanking you for is...kissing me hello. I was afraid of how things would be when you arrived today. I thought you'd come in here telling me we can't 'get close' anymore, that things would've changed overnight."

Ryan shook his head and admitted to her what he'd been forced to admit to himself. "I think I've proven I have no self-control where you're concerned. I've given up."

She grinned. "A man at my mercy. I like that."

"Be gentle," he begged, teasing.

After another kiss, though, Ryan forced his attention on her computer.

"What are you doing?"

"Reinstalling your printer," he said, finishing the short process. "Why don't you pull up your system notes and see if it works."

A moment later, the printer kicked to life and Penny's notes started filling the white pages that pushed through it. "Great," she said.

Frankly, Ryan found it unbelievable that Martin couldn't have taken care of something so simple for her. Clearly, the guy hadn't even spent five minutes looking at the problem. "You know what this means, don't you?" he asked.

"What?" She snatched up a handful of pages from the printer tray as if they were the most amazing things she'd ever seen.

"We don't have to confine ourselves to working here anymore." Of course, as recently as yesterday, his plan had been to make sure they started working in the office instead, but circumstances had changed since then. "It's a beautiful day outside," he went on. "Yesterday's rain cooled things down. I've heard a lot about Eden Park since I got here, but I haven't had the chance to check it out, even though it's just up the hill from my condo. So what do you say we take your notes and my laptop and get out in the sunshine?"

Her smile returned. "When do we leave?"

"How about as soon as your notes finish printing? I stopped by my place and threw some shorts in my briefcase, so I'll need to change."

"And I'll need my tennis shoes," she said.

Ryan headed to the bathroom to shed his suit, but he got a bit sidetracked upon stepping back into the little peach-colored room where he and Penny had been so intimate just yesterday. They were so damn good together when he let them be, that the thought filled him with warmth. He wasn't inclined to examine it too closely, but he knew he liked what he was feeling, and that he wasn't ready to let it go.

When he exited a minute later in shorts and a polo shirt, he found Penny in her bedroom, pulling her hair into a tortoiseshell barrette at the nape of her neck. "Almost ready?" he asked. The printer had quieted in the other room.

She swung open a closet door. "Just need my shoes. Can you grab a pair of white socks for me from that bottom drawer?" She pointed over her shoulder at an antique chifforobe just behind him.

"Sure." Bending to open the sock-filled drawer, Ryan grabbed the first pair of white ones his hand fell on, but what rested underneath them caught his eye. Without really thinking, he pushed aside the other socks that lay across the clear plastic container he found.

He stopped breathing when he spied, trapped within the plastic, a pair of heart-shaped handcuffs covered in red velvet. And he'd thought she was wild before? This gave a whole new meaning to the word.

Then again, this *was* the same girl who'd seduced him in a dark limousine. But, knowing her better now, Ryan couldn't resist pulling the package from the drawer, turning toward her, and clearing his throat.

When she spun to face him, the package dangled from his fingertips. "Victim of Love Handcuffs for Lovers?" he asked with one arched brow.

Penny's jaw dropped and Ryan couldn't deny enjoying her stunned expression. "That was a—a gag gift. My sister gave them to me, for some insane reason—" she gesticulated wildly "—on my twenty-fifth birthday."

"Twenty-fifth, huh? How long ago was that?"

"Almost four years."

He grinned. "Keeping them handy for some reason?"

She continued to look mortified, and Ryan mischievously took pleasure from it, until she finally let out a huge sigh. "Okay, fine, you caught me. I was cleaning out the basement a few weeks ago and found them. I guess I was sort of saving them just in case...well, you know, in case Martin..."

"Had a wild side," he finished for her.

She nodded, her pretty face nearly as red as the top she wore. "Now may I have my socks please?" She held out her hand.

"Heads up," Ryan said, tossing the balled pair of socks to her. As she caught them, he smiled, but she still looked disconcerted.

He shook his head as he dropped the handcuffs on the bed and came toward her. Although it had been fun for a minute, he didn't want her to be so embarrassed about a side of her that was so fun, so enticing. "Penny," he said, "I like it. And I really don't mind."

"Don't mind what?" she asked, exasperated.

He winked and pulled her into a warm embrace. "What an adventurous woman you are."

PENNY HAD WANTED to die when Ryan pulled those velvet handcuffs from her drawer. She'd forgotten they were even there, and now regretted putting them someplace so accessible. Of course, at the time, she'd thought she'd *wanted* them accessible, just in case anything interesting ever transpired with Martin. But thinking about that now made her want to throw the dumb things in the garbage as soon as she got home.

Thankfully, Ryan had been merciful enough not to mention them again and now they shared a lovely afternoon. First, they'd stopped at a shop in Mount Adams to grab some wine coolers and fruit to snack on. Ryan had also plucked a small bouquet of daisies from a stand of flowers, thrusting them into her fist with a wink as he told the shopkeeper to add them to the bill. He couldn't know how the small gesture had melted her heart, but she still held the flowers, even as she lay on her stomach on the blanket they'd spread next to the pond at the overlook.

Most people came to this particular spot for the view of the Ohio River wending its way through the valley below, but Penny loved the garden atmosphere, the bridge that crossed the stream leading from the pond, the large shade trees that left the grass dappled with sunlight.

"This is a nice place," Ryan said, looking up from his laptop to watch a few kids run across the bridge.

Penny lay next to where he sat, facing the other way, so she twisted her neck to see. "Yeah, Martin and I come here sometimes."

"Oh." Ryan's smile disappeared. "So then this is kind of a...special place."

Penny sighed and snapped a grape from a bunch lying on a napkin between them. "No, not really. And, as I'm realizing more every day, nothing with Martin was actually all that special. It was more like we were two friends going to the park together. Two *buddies*." She popped the grape in her mouth and stopped short of telling Ryan that today, being here with *him*, was special. In fact, she found herself noticing the park's details in a way she never had before—the ducks' wakes spreading across the water, the vibrant purple flowers that jutted from the garden to their right, and the cheerful old men with their remote control riverboats, one sporting a working calliope. Oh, she'd *seen* all of it before, but she'd never really felt it, absorbed it, the way she did right now.

"Could I have a grape?" Ryan requested, his eyes locked on the screen as he typed furiously. Penny pulled another from the bunch and lifted it to his lips. He reached out and took it with his mouth, along with her finger, which he slowly sucked from base to tip before letting go.

An unexpected bolt of pleasure shot through her, and she gave a barely-there moan.

"That's just a taste of what's to come later," he promised with one of his devilish grins. "If we can get back to work."

On that note, they dove back into the project in earnest and finished reviewing the screens he had created since yesterday. There were a lot, more than she could have imagined a single person designing in less than a day. "I can't believe how fast this is going," she mentioned offhandedly. "I thought it would take weeks to get to this point."

"Usually it might, but I guess I'm a pretty fast worker when I'm into what I'm doing." She found his boyish modesty appealing. "Of course, it'll be a while before all this is fully testable. What I'm showing you now is just to see if we're on the same page before I get it all tied together and functional. And besides, the lengthy part will be the menu and cashier systems."

But Penny barely heard the last part, because she couldn't believe what she was seeing. Was that Grace in the distance? Grace had a Scottish terrier just like the one on the woman's leash, and the woman had the same hair color and build as Martin's assistant.

Before Penny could utter a word, the woman in question turned her head, and sure enough, it was Grace.

"Uh-oh."

"Uh-oh what?" Ryan asked, still focused on the screen.

"Grace is here. Up on the sidewalk by the street."

The announcement got his full attention; he stopped typing to sneak a glance over his shoulder, then dropped his dread-filled gaze to Penny. "What on earth is she doing here?"

"Walking her dog."

"No, I mean why isn't she at work?"

Penny checked her watch. "It's almost six."

He shook his head with a sigh. "Damn it, woman, you make me lose track of time."

Penny would have enjoyed the remark more, but unfortunately, Grace's dog had just frolicked off the walkway into the grass, coming closer. Penny pulled in her breath and spoke lowly. "Don't look now, but Snowball is hunting for the perfect place to relieve himself, and he's heading our way."

8

RYAN COULDN'T BELIEVE his rotten luck. He didn't know much about the inner workings of Schuster Systems yet, but he'd already figured out that Grace was Martin's right hand around the office. "What are the chances?" he murmured, incredulous. "Of all the parks in the city, she has to choose *this* one?"

Penny ducked her head behind him slightly, then peeked around his shoulder. "Grace lives in Walnut Hills, just a few blocks from here."

He sighed, then muttered, "Great."

"I've never actually seen her here, though," she said, lifting a wary gaze. "I didn't even think about her living so close. Sorry."

Ryan nodded, trying to relax. "It's not your fault."

"Don't look so worried. After all, we're not actually doing anything wrong. We're working. You have a computer and you're keying stuff into it as we speak."

He scowled, keeping his voice low. "Penny, I don't think most system designers lie on blankets in parks with their clients while they work. With fruit and wine and flowers, no less."

Just then, a smile stretched across Penny's face when he least expected it. He didn't want to take the chance of turning his head to see why, so he said, "What is it? What's happening?"

"She's leaving."

"She is?"

"Snowball didn't find the right spot, I guess," Penny said, her tone less furtive now. "He's back on the sidewalk and they're moving past us, headed for home."

Ryan let out the huge breath he didn't even realize he'd been holding.

"I don't think she saw us," Penny added, reaching out one hand to touch his knee.

He finally looked over his shoulder to see for himself, and sure enough, he caught a last glimpse of Grace and her little white dog just before they disappeared from view behind a stand of small trees. Real relief finally washed over him, but he still wished he didn't feel as if they were hiding from a woman they both liked, a woman he knew considered Penny a friend.

"Would you be disappointed," he asked, "if I suggested we call it a day and get the hell out of here before the dog changes his mind and brings her back?"

"Not at all." Penny's tone sounded sincere, and he hoped it was, because he didn't want her to feel as if they were doing something wrong. It would be great if he could just ditch this job for her, but it wasn't that easy, as much as he hated the idea of sneaking around. Powering down his laptop, he decided to change the subject and lighten things up.

"I have to admit," he teased her, "I'm gonna miss the great view you've been giving me down your top all afternoon."

Her gaze dropped to the cleavage that had been visible ever since she'd rolled onto her stomach. Looking back up, her blue eyes widened as she smacked his thigh.

"Oh, into the rough stuff, huh? First handcuffs, now whips and chains?"

"Hey!" She rose to her knees in a show of mock outrage. "You'd better watch it."

"Or what? You'll use them on me?"

A playful chase ensued then, Ryan hopping to his feet and dashing behind an old maple tree as Penny followed. When he let her catch him, they both toppled softly to the grass, his arms falling around her waist. Her pretty eyes, her pretty mouth, lay so close that he couldn't keep from kissing her—a kiss that was short and sweet, but burned through him like fire. Afterward, their eyes met and time seemed to slow. It was as if they were speaking, whispering passionate things, even though they stayed quiet. Ryan's heart pounded and he wondered how the mood had turned so serious again that quickly.

"Uh, what happened to getting out of here?" he said, wishing his voice didn't sound so husky.

"I don't know." Hers sounded just as breathy, just as sexy.

"We should do that," he managed, gently urging her up off of him, then getting to his feet, as well.

"Right," she murmured, although she still looked equally as taken with him as he was with her.

He smiled and raised his eyebrows. "Race ya." With that, he headed back to their blanket, and soon ran toward his car lugging his briefcase, laptop and a carton of wine coolers. Penny hurried after him, toting the flowers and fruit, and dragging the old quilt she'd brought behind her.

Throwing their things into the back seat, they both got into the car breathless, although Ryan had beaten her by a mile. "You're gonna have to be a little faster," he said with a wink, "if you intend to catch me with those lovecuffs of yours."

Unfortunately, her sudden blush told Ryan that he'd just taken the joke a little too far.

"I'm only teasing, honey," he said, lifting her chin with one bent finger.

When she looked at him, he slid his arm around her and gazed into those innocent eyes. She was as shy as she was wild. It happened to be a combination that twisted his heart in a way he never could've foreseen a week ago, although he chose not to think about why.

"Come here." He leaned over the gearshift to kiss her, a kiss he wished would show her it didn't matter to him what she was—pure as the driven snow or wild as the night—but that he just liked being with her.

She returned it with a warmth that tightened his chest.

"Mmm," he said when it ended, "I wasn't teasing about that kiss, though. I say we grab some dinner, then go back to your place." He flashed a grin designed to tempt.

"On one condition."

"Anything."

"No more mention of the red-velvet you-know-whats."

He dropped a quick kiss on her forehead before easing back in his seat. "You got it."

It was only as Ryan maneuvered the car along the meandering drive that led back to the main road that he realized Penny hadn't thrown *everything* she'd been carrying into the back. The daisies he'd given her remained cradled in her arms.

Maybe the action meant nothing; maybe it just meant she liked flowers. Yet another glance made him think she was holding on to them as if they were something special, something...cherished. But hell, he'd determined before that she took sex pretty seriously, which had to mean she was taking *them*—him and her—seriously, too. Didn't it?

Well, like the Martin issue, he couldn't think about that now. It was another thing he didn't want to examine too closely, another thought to push out of his mind because it made a difficult situation easier to handle.

Just enjoy her, he told himself. Enjoy what's going on between you. Just live for right now and don't think about her heart.

And whatever you do, don't start thinking about yours, either.

HOURS LATER, Penny lay in bed, gazing up at Ryan.

Candles provided the room's only light as she lay beneath him, clad in only a pair of panties. She could see the clear outline of his erection through his boxer briefs, but enjoyed studying the rest of him, too—his broad shoulders and muscular arms, the light dusting of hair on his chest, the hungry look in his eyes as he watched her.

"Wanna do something exciting?" he suggested.

She bit her lip, nervous as usual, yet infused with the boldness that had brought her this far into the most thrilling relationship of her life. "What do you have in mind?"

"Do you trust me?"

The question caught her off guard. "Yes. Why?"

Ryan answered by gently raising her arms above her head, dropping a kiss on her waiting lips, then closing something around both her wrists before she even knew it. Leaning her head back on the pillow, she glanced up to see the heart-shaped handcuffs, the gold chain that connected them circling one of the brass bed

rails. She gasped, then looked back to him. "You promised—"

"Not to mention them. I haven't. And I won't."

She met his gaze in the candlelight, not quite sure
what to think. "But how did you...?"

"I snuck in here a little while ago and hid them under
the pillows."

"You really mean to lock me up?"

"I just did." He kissed her again. "Is that okay?"

Penny didn't know what to say. Her heart beat out of
control. She wasn't even sure what pleasure people derived from this, yet on the other hand, adventure beck-
oned, even if only timidly. "I...I guess."

"Look at it this way, honey," he whispered. "It just
means I want to be the one to do all the work here, and
give you all the pleasure. I want to excite you."

Well, *that* sounded a little too good to resist. And
minutes later, as Ryan rained scintillating kisses over
every inch of her body, Penny came to understand *exactly* what pleasure people derived from this. Placing
herself in his control was an act of complete and abiding
trust. Now she knew why he'd asked, and, oh yes, she
trusted him, more in this moment than ever before.

Of course, she remained plagued by the part of her
that couldn't quite let go of the responsible Penny, the
part that said, What on earth are you doing? But each
time, the hot sensations overrode her good girl doubts
enough that she could close her eyes and stop thinking,
stop reasoning, long enough to just feel.

Penny wasn't sure when she became aware that the
velvet cuffs were really too loose, that she could slip her
hands free if she wanted. But she ignored the knowledge and never let Ryan know, instead continuing to

bask in all the sweet and tantalizing things he did with his mouth and hands.

Just when he'd driven her to the brink of insanity, he reached above her head and freed her wrists. As her arms fell around his neck, she heard the handcuffs drop to the hardwood floor behind the bed. After that, he made love to her in the candlelight, just as slow, until their movements gradually edged into something rougher and more urgent.

They both lay recovering afterward, half-asleep and entangled in each other's arms, when Ryan whispered an accusation in her ear. "You can tell me you never fantasized about that, but I know you did."

Without opening her eyes, Penny smiled and murmured the truth. "It was just like the bathtub."

"What do you mean?"

"Better than I thought it would be."

RYAN RESTED on Penny's overstuffed couch, the candles from the bedroom now keeping the living room dimly lit and aglow. At the other end, she sat with her knees curled beneath her, her short, silky robe draping her body. He wore only underwear as they made a mismatched late-night snack of grilled cheese sandwiches, tortilla chips and wine. Penny had offered to cook something more, but he hadn't wanted to put her to any trouble, so they'd scavenged for whatever was quick and easy.

Beyond the windows and doorways, everything lay black and silent, and it seemed as if the whole world was this room, he and Penny the only people in it. That would simplify things, he thought, drawing his gaze from the flickering shadows on the walls down to the woman across from him. He felt closer to her with each passing hour, with each moment he held her, touched her, absorbed more of the sweet honesty in her eyes. And before this was over, he was going to hurt her. He knew it without a doubt.

He didn't want to think about that, but the darkness had somehow forced it to surface. What they had, no matter how good, couldn't last forever. In the end, he would jilt this beautiful, sexy, vibrant, sincere woman... for a job.

But not just a job, he reminded himself. A career. His last shot at doing something substantial and fulfilling.

"What are you thinking about?"

His eyes drifted back to the dim patterns of light dancing across the wall, but he pulled his gaze down to find Penny, an inquisitive smile gracing her face, setting her empty plate and glass aside to move closer to him on the couch. He swallowed, feeling far too serious. He didn't get serious with women often—he wasn't crazy about letting his vulnerabilities show. But then, he supposed Penny had already seen those weaknesses, more times than he could count. So hell, he thought, why not just do what *she* would do if he asked her the same question? Why not just be honest?

"I was thinking about where I've been and where I've come to." That stuff had been on his mind, as well, since it was part of the big picture here, and it would be easier than telling her he knew he was going to hurt her.

Her solemn eyes seemed to carve a path to his soul. "I know where you've come to, but I don't know the part about where you've been."

Ryan hesitated for a moment, trying to decide if he really wanted to share his thoughts, and realized he did. "I grew up in rural Indiana," he began, "home of basketball and Bible meetings."

"Did you play? And did you go?"

He grinned. "No, and no. I was the family nonconformist, the one who stood out like a sore thumb. Now my older brother, Dan, on the other hand, was the captain of the basketball team, led the youth group at church, and just for good measure, was named valedictorian of his senior class. Me, I was a good kid, but I still fell short of the mark, you know?"

She cast him a sympathetic look. "Actually, no, I'm afraid I don't. Patti would probably relate, though. We were both good kids, but I was a little more...um, the Goody Two-Shoes, I guess you might say."

He offered a wry grin. "Ironic that I would end up with the perfect one."

"Well, maybe I've been a little less perfect lately."

Ryan shook his head. "I would disagree."

They shared a warm smile until she said, "So how are things with your family now?"

He shrugged. "I'm still the nonconformist; I moved away to a white-collar world instead of staying in blue-collar Akinsville, Indiana. But I send home money every month because my parents are retired now and they need some financial help, and it's a way I can sort of...give back whatever they didn't get from me as a son."

"Ryan, I'm sure they love you and think you're a great son."

He smiled in concession. "Okay, maybe I got a little melodramatic there. Of course they love me. But I'm not sure Dan doesn't make them just a little happier than I do."

"And just where did the basketball-playing, Bible-toting valedictorian end up?"

"Right where any good basketball-playing, Bible-toting valedictorian should. Still in the heart of our hometown. He teaches English at the high school and coached the basketball team to the state championship last year. He married a perfect woman and they live in a perfect little house with two perfect children and a perfect dog. On the weekends, they drive an hour and a half to Indianapolis to do volunteer work at a homeless shelter. Carol serves up food while Dan teaches illiterate people to read."

"Wow."

He flashed a cynical look. "See what I mean? He's a hard act to follow."

"Still, Ryan, your parents have to be proud of you. Look at you, working on the cutting edge of technology, making enough money that you can send some home. It's a wonderful accomplishment."

"More wonderful, I'm afraid, when you can hold on to your jobs."

"What?"

Damn, what was he doing? Ah, hell, just telling her more of the truth, and she deserved to hear it. It would help her better understand why this had to end when the time came.

"The fact is, Penny, the reason I'm here—in Cincinnati, working for Martin—is because he liked me enough not to ask for references." From there he went on, telling her what had happened at ComData, and before that at Futureware. He meant to give her the short version, but her eyes shone with such understanding that he ended up sharing the longer one. He expected to feel humiliated when he finished, but he didn't.

"Anyway," he concluded, "that's why this job means so much to me. It feels like...a last chance. A last chance to make my parents proud and convince them I can handle the path I chose, and a last chance to make myself proud, too."

"Ah, now that part I can relate to." She reached for her wineglass and took a sip. "I felt directionless when Patti and I decided to open the pub. If it had failed, I wouldn't have known where to go, what to do, who I'd become. Before that, I'd wandered aimlessly from job to job, and I wanted more, something concrete and lasting. And even though I didn't have issues with my parents, I still wanted to make them proud."

"So maybe you understand a little more now about me coming here to settle down, wanting to walk the straight and narrow."

"Yeah," she said, looking a little guilty, although that hadn't been his intent.

"I'm not sorry, by the way. I'm not sorry about anything that's happened these last few days." In fact, Ryan was starting to have the niggling feeling that he'd gotten in too deep here. *So maybe I'm worried*, he thought, *but not sorry*.

"I'm glad," she said, gazing lovingly into his eyes. And he didn't want to see that look, but it was there, undeniably, reminding him once more how much this mattered to her. And how much it could matter to him if he let it. But he *couldn't* let it.

"So while we're on the subject of me," he joked, more than ready to take their conversation to an easy, uncomplicated place, "I need help getting another area of my life in order."

"Don't tell me there's more to your saga?" she asked with a giggle.

"Afraid so." He attempted to look very grave. "All the walls and shelves in my condo are empty. Can you help?"

She gave him a playful yet prim expression. "Well, I do consider myself a young Martha Stewart."

"I was thinking," he said, although the idea had just popped into his head, "that maybe I could talk you into helping me decorate my condo. After work tomorrow? I want the place to start looking like someone actually lives there, but I'm not really an interior decorating sort of guy. Know what I mean?" And considering all the thoughts about ending their relationship that raced through his head, the idea sounded positively ludicrous, but there it was, and he was dying for her to say yes.

"I'd love to," she said.

He smiled, already looking forward to it. "And I'd offer to make dinner for you when we're done, but I just remembered, I only have beer and butter in my refrigerator."

She smiled back. "Clearly, decorating isn't your only homemaking deficiency. Although this explains why you think grilled cheese and Doritos qualify as a meal. Why don't we hit the grocery store, too?"

"You wouldn't mind doing that with me?"

"Not at all. I'd hate to picture what you'd whip up using beer and butter."

"That would be great," he said.

So now they'd made their next plans, they knew when they'd be together again, and for Ryan, that usually meant it was a good time to call it a night. Yet it was so cozy cuddling with her on the couch, and he knew from recent experience it was even better snuggling naked with her beneath the sheets. Her eyes were so sweet peering up at him that it made it hard to leave.

"So," he said, leaning over to place a tiny kiss on the

tip of her nose, "would you care if I, uh, stayed the night?"

She shook her head lightly, spoke softly. "No, Ryan. I'd like that."

He'd suspected she would, of course, and he wished he'd done it only to please her, but he hadn't. Staying over was the one mistake he'd not committed with her so far, yet knowing he would hold her all night now and wake up to her smile in the morning made it all too easy.

FRIDAY WAS USUALLY a busy day at the Two Sisters Pub, as weekend events at the Convention Center often started then, and more people decided to eat out. Still not having heard from Martin, Penny placed one last phone call to him that morning before things got hurried, and she listened to that irritating message one final time. But tomorrow Martin would be home and phone calls wouldn't matter anymore. She wondered if this horrible waiting was karmic punishment for what she'd done while he was away.

After hanging up, though, there was little time to think about Martin, and not even much room for Ryan in her mind once the lunch rush began. Still, knowing she would see him in a couple of hours gave her an extra burst of energy. She was looking forward to their excursion tonight. Something about helping a man shop for groceries and organize his home seemed...personal. Of course, they'd already gotten more than a little personal, but to Penny, this felt as if Ryan was inviting her into his life. She had no idea how things would shake out once Martin returned, but tonight's get-together had given her hope where before there had been none, or at least only a little.

She felt bad leaving Patti, considering the lunch crowd still hadn't waned by one-thirty. But Patti assured her she had it under control and would call in an extra bartender for this evening if business warranted. Penny had told her sister what she and Ryan were doing tonight, and Patti had acted as if they were going to pick out china patterns together. "Oh, Pen, I'm so happy for you," she'd said, giving her a hug.

Ryan showed up at her house at two o'clock as scheduled, and just like every time Penny saw him, her heart nearly burst. He kissed her hello, held her close, and smiled. "So," she said, twining her arms around his neck, "is that a mouse in your pocket, or are you just glad to see me?"

Confusion shadowed his eyes. "A mouse?"

"A computer mouse," she said with a laugh.

"Ah." He leaned his head back in understanding, then laughed, too. "That's very funny, but, uh...couldn't you have picked something a little bigger?"

Grinning up at him, she tilted her head in thought. "Okay, is that a...hard drive in your pocket?"

Ryan grinned. "That's more like it, and yes, I'm *very* glad to see you."

They'd both agreed that to start working in his office at this point would still be a bad idea. Now that they had a hard copy of her notes, it might've been more convenient, but Penny worried about Martin's other employees seeing them together. She feared if they spent time in the rest of the staff's presence, they might slip up, and give away their secret.

As things were, they already knew they worked well at Penny's house, so after sharing another kiss or two, they took their respective places at Penny's desk and got down to business.

Three hours later, they'd covered a lot of ground, yet had barely made a dent in the pub's menu. "See," he said, "I told you this would be the long part."

Yet Penny didn't mind. She loved working with him, and she wouldn't complain if they never finished.

"But it's enough for today," he told her, "and besides, we've got a big night of groceries and decorating ahead of us. Still up for it?"

She nodded. "Of course."

"Then I guess I should head down to the office. The sooner I go, the sooner I can meet you at the condo." With that, he pressed his spare key into her hand and Penny closed her fist around it. He'd explained earlier that one of Martin's clients had called this morning requesting a short meeting late today, so Ryan had promised to see the guy. He'd offered to come back and pick up Penny afterward, but she'd suggested that she drive to his place on her own while he was busy, to check out the space and think about decorating possibilities before he got home.

"1201 in Adam's Landing," he reminded her. "Sure you know how to get there?"

It was one of the poshest new developments on the river. "Absolutely."

"And, uh, try not to be intimidated by all the boxes sitting around."

"Maybe I'll start unpacking some," she said, then caught herself, wondering if that was too personal an offer to make. "I mean, if you don't mind. If you'd rather I didn't—"

He shook his head. "I don't mind at all. That would be great, in fact."

"You're sure you want me snooping through your things?"

"I've got nothing to hide. No velvet handcuffs or anything like that," he said with a wink.

Penny playfully punched him in the arm, then kissed him goodbye, all the while thinking that despite her initial mortification, sharing heart-shaped handcuffs with Ryan had turned out to be incredibly sexy.

"WHAT A FABULOUS PLACE," Penny told Ryan when he arrived at his condo an hour later. She stood looking out the plate-glass window that covered the front wall of the living room, the view of the river and the bridges that crossed it almost as breathtaking as the one at the park.

"Thanks." He stepped up beside her for a moment, then turned to toss his jacket over the back of a leather recliner before loosening his tie. "It's pricy, but I like it. So, did you get any great decorating ideas?"

"Well, there's a little shop near my house with lots of candleholders and mirrors that would fit great here. After we go through your boxes and get things into place, maybe we can plan a small shopping excursion."

"Sounds good."

"By the way, I started unpacking your dishes into the cabinets. If you don't like where I put things, we can rearrange them."

He smiled. "I'm sure I'll love it. I was avoiding that job because I couldn't decide where everything should go."

"Oh, and your answering machine is blinking."

Ryan spun toward it, then pressed the playback button. "Hey, Ryan, it's your big brother. Just called to see how the new job is going. Mom said you liked it, but that you're not eating right." The brother laughed good-naturedly. "Give me a call sometime."

Ryan raised his eyebrows. "That's surprising. I hardly ever hear from Dan."

It made Penny recall the conversation they'd had about his family; she thought he had his parents pegged all wrong. "Will Dan or your mom and dad come visit? See your condo?"

He shook his head. "I doubt it. Dan and I aren't close, and Mom and Dad are basically homebodies, not into long car trips or big cities. And they'd probably find this place a little extravagant. They like simpler things."

"So do I," she reminded him. "But this place is wonderful."

"Still, like I told you, my parents and I are worlds apart. They're in the old world and I'm in the new. They have very old-fashioned values."

She flinched at the words, surprised at how hard the thought of being "old-fashioned" struck her.

"What's wrong?"

She sighed. "Well, until a few weeks ago I guess I thought of *myself* as someone with old-fashioned values. But now..."

Ryan gave her a scolding smile, then pulled her down onto the dark, leather sofa. "It's okay to be versatile, Penny. It's okay to have your own ideas and feelings about things."

"But when I imagine the looks on my parents' faces if they could see what we've been..."

He tilted his head. "You're not *supposed* to imagine that, honey. Don't go there. As long as the things you do feel right to *you*, then that's right enough."

Penny considered what he'd said. She wasn't sure how she'd ended up on this ride where one minute she was announcing how wanton and sexually free she was and the next, recanting, worrying about it. She supposed it was just a difficult transition for the ultimate good girl to make. Yet Ryan was going through it with her. He had started exploring her fantasies with her just as she'd dreamed, and now he was helping her get her emotions in place, too.

"Maybe you'd do well to remember those words yourself, Mr. Pierce," she said, thinking of all he'd shared with her last night.

He gave her a knowing smile. "Okay, are we talking about my parents, or are we talking about me, you and Martin?"

"I don't know. Maybe all of it. Maybe we should all just be a little more trusting of our feelings sometimes."

"And not worry about who gets hurt or what anyone thinks of us?"

"I didn't say *that*. But I think there must be a happy medium, and the trick in life is finding it."

Ryan simply nodded, but where he and Penny were concerned, he didn't know how they were going to reach any such ideal medium. He understood how what she was saying applied to his relationship with his parents—that if he liked his life and knew he'd done his best, that should be enough. He also understood how it applied to her recent self-discoveries—if she liked herself, that was all that mattered. But when Martin entered the picture, things weren't nearly so cut-and-dried.

"Well," he said, having had enough of this inner contemplation, "as soon as I get changed, we can venture out to the store."

"I checked out your fridge and pantry," she told him as he got to his feet. "You've got a lot of room, so we can stock up and you shouldn't have to do this again for a while."

He grinned down at her. "I've said it before and I'll say it again—you're a woman after my own heart."

It was a revelation that was starting to trouble him, he realized as he made his way to the bedroom. After waking up to her pretty eyes and tousled hair this morning, he'd thought about her as he'd driven home to shower, then all day at the office, too. He'd even found himself popping into the lobby for no good reason around lunchtime, hoping to catch her daily sandwich delivery, but he'd missed it.

And the sex. Every single time it blew his mind. He never got used to the way it felt to be inside her, the way his soul ached when she moaned for him. Even just kissing her made him feel like a lovesick teenager.

So much for settling down in Cincinnati, he thought, as he slid a burgundy polo shirt over his head. But then, if not for the wild parts, and if not for the risk factors, he supposed this could feel quite settled. Once they got past the sexual frustration, everything with her had come so easy—relaxing in the park together, eating together, talking in bed, even telling her about his parents and Dan, and about losing his job at ComData. Every time they were apart, Ryan found himself thinking about her, looking forward to the moment they'd see each other again.

And now they were going grocery shopping. It sounded ridiculously domestic, but he was looking forward to it.

Tucking his shirt into a pair of faded blue jeans, Ryan sighed, ran a hand through his hair, then glanced at himself in the mirror.

You, he thought, had better get control of this situation. Soon. Before it all blows up in your face.

RYAN PUSHED THE CART, which overflowed with everything from milk and eggs to a variety of frozen foods. "Hey, look. Goetta," Penny said, pointing to the sign on one of the refrigerated bins. "Want some?"

"*Goetta?* What is it?"

"Oh," Penny said, "I guess it's one of those regional foods. It's...um, kind of a sausagey, oatmealy sort of thing."

Ryan laughed. "No thanks." Penny had been a huge help to him so far and made this task much more fun than it would have been otherwise, but every now and then she tried to get him to buy something that just wasn't on his personal menu.

She turned to face him from the other end of the stopped cart. "Are you sure? You can do a lot of good stuff with goetta."

"No goetta," he said with a decisive point of his finger. "I mean it. I just don't think I'm a goetta guy." Prior to this, he'd also had to convince her he wasn't a ricecake or hummus guy.

Before she could protest further, he backed the cart away from her, then swung it down the next aisle. Glass-fronted freezers filled with ice cream spanned its length. "Now, this is more like it," he murmured, studying his choices, then grabbing tubs of French vanilla, cookies-n-cream, and double chocolate.

Penny leaned around to pat his stomach. "I can't believe you maintain this with these kinds of shopping habits."

"I won't be back for a while, remember? This is a stock-up trip."

"Ooh," she said then, stepping past, her focus having shifted to something behind him. "Hot fudge."

Ryan turned to find her examining a shelf of ice-cream condiments, and he witnessed a familiar and all-too alluring look in her eyes before she caught him watching, then lowered her gaze. Considering how well he was beginning to know her in certain ways, he understood exactly what that look meant. He arched one eyebrow and grinned.

"What?" she asked.

But those innocent eyes weren't working on him this time. "You've got a hot fudge fantasy. Don't deny it."

She gasped. "I..." She shook her head helplessly. "How did you..." Then she gave it all up. "Oh, darn it, all right, I do. So sue me."

Ryan smiled in triumph. "And you can't even blame this one on Patti."

Penny's blue eyes went wide. "She *did* buy me those things. I swear it."

He laughed, realizing he loved teasing her way too much, then stepped up close to her in the aisle, which was desolate except for them. "You should quit being so defensive. It just so happens..."

"What?"

She peered up at him as he cast his most suggestive grin. "That I have a hot fudge fantasy, too." Or at least he did now.

He enjoyed seeing the shock on her face melt into something a little more lurid as he reached past her, tossing two jars of the microwavable hot fudge into the cart.

She glanced down at where they lay atop a bunch of canned goods. "But, uh, don't you think that's a lot?"

He shrugged, then dropped a playful kiss on her cheek. "Anything left over can go on the ice cream."

BACK AT RYAN'S, they filled his refrigerator and pantry with groceries, then Penny showed him how she'd arranged his cabinets. After unloading some glasses, pots and pans, and a few dish towels, the kitchen was quite livable. "See how fast that went with your guidance?" he said. Then he placed his hand on the back of her neck and pulled her in for a kiss. "Thank you for helping me."

After that, they worked in the living room. When Penny had arrived, only basic furniture and the big screen TV had been in place, and a pile of boxes had waited in one corner. Within half an hour, lamps dotted the room, pillows and a throw made the couch cozier, and she had found some candles that added character to the coffee table. Next, she put Ryan to work hooking up his VCR and stereo while she started filling the built-in, mirrored shelves with books and bric-a-brac, including a couple of framed photos she'd unpacked.

One of the photos captured four guys with backpacks and sleeping bags standing in front of an SUV. When she held it up, Ryan explained that he and his college buddies always got together for a hiking trip every fall. They were scattered across the country now, but that was the one time they all got together each year.

The other picture was a family photo, although she didn't call this one to Ryan's attention. In it, the Pierces and their two grown boys stood next to a Christmas tree, Ryan's father spreading his arms around each of his sons. They looked like very nice people, although she had to admit Ryan was right—he stood out in the crowd. He was taller and broader than his father or brother, somehow appeared more rugged and masculine. She couldn't believe he didn't know what an amazing man he was.

She turned to watch him fiddling with wires and cables on the carpet not far away, and thought about his belief that his parents didn't care much about him. As her heart filled with emotion for him, she almost said *I love you*, because she really thought it might be true—it felt that way more and more all the time—and she wanted him to know.

Thank God she realized it was the move of a lunatic before she actually did it.

"What's up?" he asked, catching her look.

"Just wondering how it's coming over there."

He laughed. "I know it seems like a mess right now, but five minutes, and I'll have it up and running."

"What's next?" she asked, done with the shelves.

"You wanna order a pizza or something? I don't know the good places around here yet."

"One LaRosa's pizza, coming up." Penny tossed her empty boxes in a pile next to the wall-spanning window en route to the phone, but the view stopped her progress. Outside, darkness hovered and the sunset glowed magnificently over the river. Streaks of electric pink blazed across the horizon to the west, and tiny dots of light sprinkled the hills below that led down to the Ohio. "Oh, Ryan, come look at this. Is it like this every night from up here?"

He joined her, sliding his arms around her waist from behind. "I don't really know. I'm usually working or having fun with you this time of night," he said, sounding playful. "But it's pretty great, isn't it?" He leaned forward, dropping one delicate kiss on her neck as they took in the spectacular colors, streaks of plum now twining their way through the pink splash of sky.

"So what do you wanna do after we eat pizza?" she whispered up to him.

"Easy," he growled. "Break into the hot fudge and have you for dessert."

"WE'RE A MESS," Penny sighed as she kissed him.

"I know." He reached to wipe off the remnants of chocolate that had somehow ended up on her cheek.

"I'm exhausted." She reached to kiss him once more.

"You wore me out, too."

They lay in Ryan's bed on sheets he'd promised were old, and thank goodness, because they'd never be the same again. Penny didn't think hot fudge would ever *taste* quite the same to her again, either.

"I should shower," she suggested.

"Afraid you'll have to wash your hair while you're at it." He ran his fingers down a long lock now caked with partially dried fudge.

Suddenly amused almost beyond her comprehension, Penny rolled over on her back and started laughing.

He smiled down on her in the lamplight. "What?"

"I can't believe we just did that." It had been so freeing, so sensual, and so incredibly easy.

"Oh, come on," he teased. "Considering some of the other stuff we've done over the past week, what's a little hot fudge?"

She smiled up at him, then used her thumbnail to chip away a tiny blot of dry chocolate from his chin. "It was fun, wasn't it?"

"The hot fudge? Or everything else, too?"

"The hot fudge," she said. The warm sensation of

having it dribbled over her and then watching him lick it off had been nothing less than exquisite. "But everything else, too."

"Starting a week ago tonight," he said, and Penny shook her head in disbelief. She couldn't believe they'd gotten together only a week ago! But then again, given *how* they'd gotten together, maybe what'd followed had been somehow inevitable, meant to be. "It's been one hell of a week," he added, nuzzling her ear, then softly biting her neck.

"I was just thinking the same thing."

I love you.

The words had struck her in an undeniable way as she and Ryan had made love and, suddenly, not a shred of doubt remained. When she'd heard his deep moan and felt his body collapsing against her, she'd realized how profoundly she cherished bringing him pleasure and she'd known, just known beyond question, that it was indeed love.

She couldn't tell him, of course, since nothing had really changed between them except for what rested in her heart. But it was real and solid and surrounded Penny like a warm cocoon she could never escape from, could never *want* to escape from.

She wasn't afraid anymore, or nervous about anything they did together. She had moaned and laughed and relished every moment of living out her hot fudge fantasy with Ryan. Not one scrap of guilt or "good-girlness" had snuck in. She'd simply been having decadent fun with the man she loved, nothing more, nothing less. It was as if realizing she truly loved him had cleared her head in other ways, too, freed her from the chains she'd locked herself in somewhere along the way.

And best of all, none of this was startling. She knew they hadn't known each other very long, yet it seemed as if they had, as if all the feelings had been growing in her from the moment they'd met. Now love was blooming inside her, and she just wanted to bask in it, like a spring flower in the sun.

A few minutes later, she watched Ryan drag himself up from the chocolate-stained sheets to make his way to the shower, both of them laughing again at what a mess they were. He soon returned from the bathroom with a large navy blue bath sheet hooked at his waist. "Shower's free if you're recovered enough," he said with a wink.

"I'm getting there," she sighed happily.

"While you're getting cleaned up," he said with a laugh, "I'll get these sheets off the bed and into the washing machine before I end up tracking chocolate footprints through the condo."

Soon after, they lay back down together, both wrapped in navy towels, on Ryan's leather couch, laughing still more because he hadn't had any luck locating clean sheets. Penny wanted to spend all night in his arms, and she hardly cared if it was in a bed or on the couch or on the floor.

"I guess Martin never returned your calls or you'd have mentioned it," he said as she settled into his arms.

"No, he didn't, and I don't understand why. But I suppose that doesn't matter now."

"Why not?"

"He'll be home tomorrow," she said. "So maybe I was meant to tell him face-to-face."

As his body tensed beneath her, she gazed down at him in the darkened room, lit only by the glow from the city below gleaming through the large window. She couldn't make out his expression, but she sensed his surprise at the reminder and her chest tightened.

Just then, the phone rang across the room. Ryan made no move to get it, so they both lay there, listening as the answering machine picked up.

"Hello, Ryan, it's your mother. I'm calling with some good news about Dan. I ran into Ellen Winston at the beauty parlor and she let out a secret—the alumni association at the high school is planning to give your brother a lifetime achievement award this fall! He'll be the youngest recipient in the school's history! Be sure not to breathe a word, though, since it'll be a surprise at the alumni banquet. Call me and I'll fill you in on the details. Bye." The answering machine went quiet before clicking off.

Penny heard Ryan's sigh beneath her and they started talking at the same time.

"Ryan, they—"

"I hate to—"

They both stopped.

"You first," she said.

She heard him take a deep breath. The room seemed too quiet. She waited, but he didn't reply, although his heartbeat sped up beneath her palm.

"What is it?" she whispered.

"I was just thinking," he began, "that maybe we should, uh...take a little break from each other."

A huge knot formed in her stomach.

"Since Martin's coming back tomorrow," he went on. "Just until you get a chance to talk to him and we see how it goes. You know?"

Penny's breath felt shaky and she inhaled, then exhaled, trying to smooth it out. This is a fling. Just a fling. At least that's what it is to him. She had to remember that and deal with it. She had to forget the love pounding in her chest and seeping through her pores.

"Yeah," she finally said. "That would probably make sense." As much as she hated it, it *did* make sense because Martin could show up at her place, or see them out somewhere together, and neither she nor Ryan wanted him to find out what'd been going on. It had been easy to push aside thoughts of Martin while he was away, but she didn't want to hurt him, had never wanted to hurt him. And she *did* need time to deal with how she was going to say no to Martin's proposal. So it made perfect sense.

Only the thought of being apart from Ryan broke her heart.

So much for loving Ryan. And so much for an invitation into his life. Instead, the night had turned into an invitation *out* of it.

9

RYAN HAD KNOWN Martin was due back a week after he'd left, of course, but somehow it hadn't quite sunk in that it was *now*. Penny's words, "He'll be home tomorrow," had been like a cold glass of water splashing him in the face. A wake-up call. A huge sign that read, Think About Your Future, bashing him over the head. The timing of his mother's phone message hadn't helped, either.

He only wished he didn't see the hurt in Penny's eyes. "I have plenty to stay busy with," he went on, anxious to fill the sudden void. Funny how shared silence could be so nice one minute, yet so awkward the next. "As I said, the food order part of the system will be the most time-consuming on my end. So let's plan on, uh, not getting together in the afternoons until you hear from me, okay?"

"Okay," she said. But her voice was far too soft and it made his heart clench.

This was it, that moment he'd dreaded, the moment where he hurt her.

He wished he could do something to stop what was happening. But when he realized Martin would really be back tomorrow, back in her life and back in his, he knew the fantasies were over, at least for a while.

He didn't know what else to say and wished he'd been better prepared and realized Martin's return was coming so fast. Her body had gone rigid in his arms, and he gently stroked her soft shoulders, hoping somehow to soothe her, to let her know this wasn't how he really wanted things.

Then he realized he could tell her that, in the hopes it would help. It was something anyway. "This isn't how I want things to be, Penny. You know that, don't you? You know I wish things were different."

"Of course."

He sensed how strong and agreeable she was trying to be, but heard the underlying sadness in her voice just the same.

He squeezed her tight, just wanting to feel her, and let her know he cared. This was hard for him, too. When he lifted slightly to kiss her forehead, she pulled away.

She was off the couch, free of his embrace, before he even knew what'd hit him.

"Penny, where are—" The lamp she turned on blinded him and he held a hand up to shield his eyes, squinting at her as she moved through the living room. She held her big navy towel closed as she stooped to snatch up the clothes she'd shed earlier before even making it to the bed.

"I'm gonna head home," she said without looking at him, obviously struggling to sound casual as she slid her panties on without dropping the towel.

"Penny—" he rose on one elbow to look at her "—you don't have to go."

Letting the towel fall to her feet, she kept her back to him as she hooked her bra and slid the straps onto her shoulders.

"I know," she said, turning to face him as she reached for her shorts. She forced a smile, trying her best to look pleasant. "But I'm tired and it's late and...well, maybe it's best, all things considered."

Ryan sighed and got to his feet, fastening his towel at his waist as he neared her.

She pulled her T-shirt over her head.

Stopping in front of her, he ran a hand through his hair and felt like the ass of the century. "I really know how to ruin a nice evening, don't I?"

"You didn't ruin it." She shook her head insistently. "And I understand. You're right about this." Rising up on her tiptoes, Penny kissed his cheek, then moved past him toward the door, grabbing her purse on the way.

Ryan followed, thinking he should do something, not let her leave this way, but no words of protest ever left his mouth, and within seconds, Penny was disappearing out his door and up the hall toward the elevator.

He stood in the doorway after she'd gone, realizing he hadn't even said goodbye. An enormous emptiness washed through him when he heard the elevator ding around the corner, when he knew he'd really let her leave without doing a damn thing to prevent it.

But he'd known it would come to this. He'd known it would have to. And surely she had, too, hadn't she?

Shaking his head in regret, he stepped back inside and shut the door. This would all be okay in the end. It would have to be, because he'd had no other choice. And it wasn't as if he'd told her he didn't want to be with her or thrown her out on the street. He'd just made a move that seemed sensible for them both.

And as for what this weekend would be like without her, well, it would be like all the *other* weekends he'd ever spent without her—no big deal. He was a self-reliant guy, the type who didn't mind moving to a strange city without any friends, who liked people but didn't tend to get deeply attached.

So why couldn't he remember a moment when he'd ever felt so lonely?

RYAN SPENT most of Saturday at Schuster Systems, working on the Two Sisters project. He no longer used Martin's office, not just because his own computer had arrived, but because Martin was his boss, the corner office belonged to him, and Ryan wanted to make damn sure he remembered that. Squeezing himself into his own matchbox-size office seemed a good way to get the idea through his head once and for all.

If you wanted to go places in a company, you started at the bottom and paid your dues. And you followed the rules, both the written and unwritten ones, specifically, Don't have sex with the woman the boss wants to marry and Don't keep doing it over and over. Ryan was going to start paying attention to the pecking order here, staying in his place and keeping his nose to the grindstone, being that "good boy" he'd once told Penny he'd come here to be.

He sank into the work for long stretches and let it remind him how much he loved what he did. He was a damn good system designer and it always showed in the finished product. It also temporarily got his mind off of *her.*

Of course, all that changed every time he stopped to go to the bathroom or get something to drink from the kitchen, as he was doing now. He stood before a snack machine perusing chocolate bars and, not surprisingly, they automatically turned his mind to Penny. But then, so did a lot of other things these days. Limousines, bathtubs, bras. *Feet,* for God's sake! And now chocolate. Finally deciding the thought of chocolate without her underneath it sounded unbearable, he chose peanut-butter crackers instead.

Snatching up the package from the machine's bin, then grabbing a soft drink, he made his way back toward his office. Damn, he thought, that'd been bad timing last night. He rolled his eyes, remembering what he'd done. Nice, Ryan, real nice. Slather the girl in hot fudge, make love to her like there's no tomorrow, then toss her out of your life. He didn't think he'd ever done anything so cold, although it hadn't seemed that way at the time. He'd kept thinking *sensible, sensible, sensible,* but today, it just seemed *cold.*

This was all Martin's fault. He wanted to believe that as he caught sight of the man's name on the office door down the hall.

But no. This was all *Ryan's* fault. For needing Schuster Systems so badly. For screwing up all his other chances. No one was to blame but him.

It would serve him right if Penny forgot all about turning down Martin's proposal and married him anyway. Of course, she'd said there was nothing real between her and Martin, but what if she'd exaggerated, merely been swept up in passion? What if there *was* something between them? And what if it appeared a hell of a lot better to her right now than Ryan did? After all, look at all Martin could offer her. For one thing, stability. Then there was financial security *and* a lasting commitment.

Ryan let out a cynical laugh as he settled behind his desk. Ironic that stability was the one thing *he* craved—he wanted a job that would last, a life that felt comfortable and dependable—yet it remained the one thing he couldn't even begin to offer Penny.

Nonetheless, the idea gave him pause, halting him in mid-keystroke. Was that what he wanted? To offer her stability?

The very notion gave him that familiar feeling he got whenever she was around, for the first time since she'd walked out his door last night. He'd thought he was taking control of the situation by putting distance between them, but suddenly he feared he'd let her get even further out of his grasp. At least when they'd been together, he'd known that part of his life was good and secure.

He took a deep breath and ran his hand through his hair, realizing he'd never felt quite so secure in his life as he had with Penny. She was always so honest, so sweet, so affectionate. He'd never had to worry that she'd suddenly leave him, because she always wanted him to stay. He'd never had to fear that she wanted him to change, wanted *anything* to change, because he'd seen in her eyes and felt in her touch that she liked him just as he was. She didn't care about his past or even if he had a questionable future. She just liked him. *More* than liked him. He had seen that and couldn't deny it. She cared for him...and, damn it, he cared for her, too.

He...*loved* her.

What else could make his heart hurt so bad right now? What else could have him risking his career over a touch, a kiss, an embrace?

It was true. *He was in love with Penny Halloran.*

And he'd pretty much thrown her out of his life.

PENNY HAD WAITED all day on Saturday to hear from Martin. When afternoon had ebbed into evening, she'd called him at home...and gotten yet another recorded message. "You've reached Martin Schuster of Schuster

Systems. I'm not available to take your call, but if you leave your name and number, I'll get back to you. Or you can try reaching me at my office..." She'd hung up in total frustration. What on earth was going on here? Where *was* he?

Now it was Sunday afternoon and she was nearly out of her head.

"Let's go shopping," Patti said, standing in Penny's foyer.

"Shopping?" Penny had just filled her sister in on the latest turn of events, including that she still hadn't talked to Martin and that her love life was in shambles. "I'm hardly in the mood for shopping."

"Oh, come on. A little shopatherapy always does a girl good. We'll buy you something new to wear, something sexy, something to reflect the new you."

Penny only sighed. "I'm hardly in the mood to be sexy. After all, I don't have anyone to be sexy *with* anymore."

Patti raked a dismissing hand down through the air. "Details, details." She grabbed Penny's wrist in one hand and scooped up Penny's purse in the other. "Come on. I'll drive."

After Patti dragged her from the house, Penny dug in her purse for her keys. As she locked the door, though, she glanced down to see Ryan's spare condo key still hanging from the ring, which only added to her depression.

"I'm so sorry you have to go through this," her sister said, apparently realizing just how deep Penny's despair ran.

"There's no one to blame but myself. This is what I get," she told Patti as they started down the front walk, "for not making sure Martin knew how I felt before moving on. I deserve this."

"No, you deserve Ryan. Although I'm considering kicking his butt right now."

Penny shook her head as they approached Patti's car. "He's just trying to save his job. You can't blame the guy for that."

"Yes, I can. Some things are more important."

"I never asked him for promises," she said, peering at her sister over the roof of the car just before they got inside. "I never asked him for anything more than a good time, fun, sex." She stopped then, turning to gape at her sister in pure horror. "Oh God, I'm a good-time girl! I have indiscriminate sex with strangers! I treat sex like it's nothing!"

Patti tilted her head. "Did it feel like that, Pen? Did it feel like nothing?"

Penny thought all the way back to her first meeting with Ryan in the limo, and then to everything after. "Never," she said quietly. And then she admitted one more thing to her sister. "I'm in love with him."

"Ah." Patti cast her a consoling glance, after which she started the car and pulled away from the curb. "Well, then, rest assured, you're not a good-time girl. Your only crime is falling in love with a guy who isn't ready to give it back."

"And just what am I supposed to do about that?"

Patti shrugged. "Picking up a cute miniskirt couldn't hurt."

ON MONDAY MORNING, Ryan kept his office door wide open, listening. It would happen any minute now—the elevator would ding, the doors would slide open, and Martin's voice would echo through the hallways of

Schuster Systems. He would greet Grace, make small talk about his conference, catch up on important messages, then shuffle past Ryan's closet, maybe pausing for a hello. Ryan's heart rose to his throat each time he heard the elevator stop on his floor.

When Martin hadn't arrived by nine, Ryan thought he must be sleeping in. But when he still hadn't shown up by ten, Ryan started getting antsy.

He needed Martin to show up. He needed to get his life back to normal. He needed to know Penny had talked to him, to somehow find out what she'd said and how it had gone.

Half an hour later, the office remained quiet, everyone working at their various tasks, but still no Martin. Was Ryan the only one to notice his absence? Did everyone else know where Martin was and had just neglected to tell *him*?

Clicking the save icon on his computer screen, Ryan made his way to the lobby. Grace looked up from opening the mail when he stopped at her desk. "Yes?"

"I was just wondering about Martin. Isn't he due back today? I haven't seen him."

"He's not back in town yet."

Ryan felt his blood pressure begin to spike. "He's not back? Why not? Do you have any idea?"

Grace gave him the same look one might cast upon a suspected mental ward escapee. "Don't get upset, Ryan. He'll be back."

Don't get upset? *Don't get upset?*

But he had to keep his emotions under control. They were showing way too much and Grace clearly thought he was going insane. And the fact was, he was starting to *feel* a little crazy upon realizing he'd just spent a weekend apart from Penny for apparently no reason at all.

"I just...need to talk to him about some projects," he said, working to keep his voice even. "I was anxious for his return."

"Well, he called just a little while ago."

"What did he say?"

Grace turned her attention back to the mail. "He couldn't talk long, but wanted to tell me he'd been delayed. He said he'd call again tomorrow to let me know when he'd be home."

"Well...what do you think is keeping him?"

Grace lifted her gaze once more, clearly getting frustrated. "Could be a lot of things. Most likely, some business opportunity came up that couldn't wait."

Ryan nodded and tried to act as if that was a good enough answer, but no matter what was holding Martin in Vegas, Ryan was starting to think it damned irresponsible of him. He had a business to run. Messages were piling up. And for God's sake, he'd asked a woman to marry him who was waiting to give him an answer! What kind of a man *was* this?

And to think Ryan had lost his last job for showing up somewhere ninety minutes late!

He made his way back to his desk and returned to work, but when noon arrived and still his bones ached with missing Penny, he threw down his pencil and got to his feet. This was it! He was taking action.

For one thing, he couldn't live with the fact that he'd hurt her. For another, he was beginning to think he had his priorities screwed up. Not to mention that he was confused as hell about his recent realization that he was in love with her.

No wonder he was acting so ridiculous; part of him

remained concerned about his job, while another part was starting to think about some impossible, improbable future, and he'd even started worrying about her wild side. What if he was wrong and she *didn't* feel the same way he felt about her? What if she realized she wanted to have fun, live the single life? Maybe Penny wouldn't even *want* anything long-term.

Oh hell, nothing made sense to him anymore, and this new fear just complicated things even further.

"I'm going out for a while," he told Grace as he headed toward the elevator. He had to get out of the office before he lost his mind.

"I already ordered your sandwich. Do you still want it?"

"Yeah, I'll eat when I get back. I just need to run an errand."

Getting off the elevator and moving through the revolving door onto Walnut Street a minute later, Ryan hit the sidewalk toward the Tower Place Mall. What he planned to do wouldn't even begin to help his confusion or solve their problems, but at least it would let Penny know she was on his mind, and that he wanted her desperately.

PENNY WENT THROUGH the workday in a daze. They were busy for a Monday, and she kept up with the pub's traffic, but she barely remembered what she was doing from one moment to the next. When she left a little before five, she was exhausted, although she knew it was more mental than physical. Martin's unexplained absence was eating at her, and Ryan's *explained* absence was killing her.

Maybe Patti had been right. Maybe her only crime was falling for a guy who couldn't return her feelings no matter how wonderful things seemed when they were together. So she tried not to concentrate on memories of their shared laughter, their sweet quiet moments, their lovemaking, and instead attempted to focus on the fact that none of it had been enough to win his love.

After Patti's relentless prodding, Penny *had* returned home with a new miniskirt yesterday, her first ever. She'd also picked up a couple of tops that were more formfitting than the clothes she usually wore. She had actually enjoyed their spree, and even liked the idea of wearing her new purchases; she was used to wearing flirty stuff underneath her clothes, but wearing it on the outside would be a new thing for her—other than the night of the limo encounter, of course. The only problem was, she wasn't sure she'd feel comfortable wearing her new clothes for anyone, with anyone, but Ryan.

Swinging the car into the driveway, she dragged herself over the lawn and into the house. As she thumbed through her mail, she noticed her answering machine was blinking and absently reached to press the playback button. When she heard Martin's voice, she dropped the mail on the counter and stared at the phone.

"Penny, it's Martin. Forgive me for not calling sooner—time has gotten away from me here. I wish you were home; I'd hoped we could talk." He paused then, sighing. "Well, as you know by now, I've been delayed, but I'll be back soon, and you'll be hearing from me."

When the machine clicked off, Penny just kept staring at it. She was glad he'd finally called, but his vague message about being delayed left her even *more* frustrated. This meant he wouldn't be home tonight, just as he hadn't been home all weekend. And for all she knew, he wouldn't come home for days yet. Something in his voice had sounded so cryptic that it added to her feelings of disappointment. Why hadn't he said when he was coming back? Why hadn't he mentioned what the holdup was?

When the doorbell interrupted her thoughts, Penny shifted her thoughts away from Martin as best she could to find a deliveryman waiting on her front porch. After signing and accepting the small package—a pretty little box covered in tiny red hearts with a red-foil bow on top—she shut the door and looked at it. "What on earth...?"

Thoughts skittered through her head. Had Patti sent her something to cheer her up? No, if her sister had wanted to give her a gift, she'd have done it at the restaurant, or yesterday when they'd shopped together. And then it hit her. Martin. This was some sort of combination romance/apology/explanation present. He'd said she'd be hearing from him and maybe this was what he'd meant.

Penny untied the bow, letting the ribbon drop to the floor, then removed the lid. Nestled in a bed of red tissue paper lay a skimpy, flirty pair of tiger-striped thong panties with a scalloped edge. Oh my. This was from *Martin?*

But slowly, warily, another possibility began to nudge its way into her mind as she reached for the card inside.

To the woman who brings out the animal in me. I miss you. Ryan.

Penny went as weak as a kitten, even as her heart pounded out of control. She remembered wanting to bring out the animal in Martin, and instead it had happened with someone else.

Oh God, she loved him. With all her aching heart.

She wasn't even sure exactly what the panties meant, if anything had really changed, but...maybe she could *make* them change.

RYAN HAD PLANNED to leave the office by six, anxious to get home to see if a message from Penny might be waiting on his answering machine. If not, he'd thought he might call her or drive by her house to see if she'd gotten his gift, and to see if she hated him or if the gesture had managed to smooth things over at all.

But when Ryan checked Martin's e-mail right before leaving, he found one that had to be dealt with, which meant so much for leaving by six. A client in California was having system problems and Ryan didn't know if he could help, but felt obligated to call him anyway, especially since it was only three o'clock there.

Two hours later, he hung up the phone. It had taken a while, but he'd figured out the problem and walked the guy through fixing it. After turning off the last light in the office, he made his way up a now empty Fourth Street toward his parking garage. And even if he didn't feel great about much else in his life at the moment, he at least knew he'd put in a good, hard day's work.

The sun was sinking over the river by the time he got out of his car, the Daniel Beard bridge silhouetted in the forefront, and it made him think of Penny and the sunset they'd shared just a few nights ago. Strange, it seemed more like an eternity.

He wondered if it was too late to go see her now, knowing she must have gotten her surprise by this time. His skin prickled with uncharacteristic nervousness as he tried to imagine her reaction. He felt like a kid who'd just sent his first love note.

Stepping into the condo, dark but for the pink glow of sky blazing through the huge living room window, he flipped on an overhead light. He'd been just about to swing his briefcase onto the kitchen counter when he stopped, his eyes drawn to a piece of paper he hadn't put there, a note written in red ink.

Come to the bedroom, Tiger.

10

RYAN STOPPED in the bedroom doorway, stunned by the sight before him. Penny stood against the open balcony door, arms stretched above her head, wearing nothing but the tiger-striped panties he'd sent her.

The first seductive notes of Al Green's "Let's Stay Together" wafted from the radio by the bed. Penny's hair spilled over her shoulders in dark blond waves, framing her pretty face and the rounded breasts below, their pink crests beaded. Her hips flared slightly from her narrowed waist, the small swath of tiger print stretching across them. With the white sheers fluttering around her in the breeze, she looked like a flesh-and-blood sex goddess, something he might've dreamed.

But he wasn't dreaming. This was real. *She* was real. He let his briefcase drop to the floor.

"Hello there," she said in a breathy voice that added to his arousal.

"Uh, hi. I see you, uh, got my..."

She gave him a provocative nod. "Do you like?"

"Yeah," he said, adding a deeper, "Oh yeah," as her hips began to sway in slow rhythm with the music. "Uh, how did you..."

She kept the sexy voice. "I forgot to return your key."

"I'm glad."

"Me, too," she whispered, but then the sensual look

in her eyes softened as her hips stilled. "I missed you, Ryan."

Her words pierced his heart as it beat out of control, not just with arousal now, but so much more.

He finally left the doorway and went to her. She was so beautiful he almost couldn't bear to touch her, to mar the perfect image before him, to let the moment end. Yet, tentatively, he lifted both hands to her face, then gave her a slow, lingering kiss. When he pulled back, she looked as awed by his tenderness as he was. His whole body thrummed with emotion...with love. She was his sun and moon, his day and night, his sweet, innocent sandwich girl and his hot, daring sex kitten.

He touched her lips with two fingertips. "I've missed your kisses."

A familiar look of romantic desperation grew in her eyes just before Penny threw her arms around his neck, clinging to him. He savored how much she needed him, knowing now what should've been apparent from the beginning—he needed her just as much.

When next their lips met, they traded kisses filled with more urgency than he'd ever known, and his hands roamed her tantalizing curves as she worked to get him out of his clothes. Soon he stood naked before her, his arousal brushing her stomach as he drank in the heat that burned in her eyes.

"Lie down," she said.

The command caught him so off guard he merely gaped.

"Remember the night when you did all the work and gave me all the pleasure?"

He nodded, letting her back him onto the bed.

"Well," she said, coming to kneel over him, "I want to return the favor."

He rested his head on the feather pillow, watching as Penny hovered above him, her breasts suspended mere inches over his face. He thought to lift his head enough to nip at one of them, to get one sweet taste of her, when he heard something click—twice—and realized his wrists were encircled with plush fabric.

He knew before he even looked up that she'd hooked him to the wrought iron that lined the top of his sleigh bed with the velvet handcuffs. A laugh erupted from his throat, yet his amusement quickly dissolved into a look of pure sexuality he hoped she felt to her core. "Maybe I was wrong," he said. "Maybe *you're* the animal."

"I think we both are; that's why we go together so well." She gave him a suggestive smile. "Although I should warn you, you ain't seen nothin' yet."

With that, Penny lowered a soft kiss to his lips, then took one last look into his eyes before proceeding downward. She rained kisses onto his neck, his shoulders, his chest, each vibrating through him like the gentle but potent strum of a harp. "You're so sweet," he murmured as her kisses moved lower over his stomach, making the muscles in his groin pull taut.

He let out a soft moan, still watching her every move as his pleasure began to mix with an almost painful anticipation. He groaned just thinking about, imagining... And then her soft hand wrapped around his hardness, stroking him lightly. "Ah..." he sighed as her perfect touch pulsed through him.

"I want to make you feel incredible," she said, lifting her eyes to his once more as she lowered a delicate kiss to the tip of his arousal. A moan tore from deep in his chest, his entire body tensing with heat and something that felt almost like gratification, except it begged for more.

She took him into her mouth, her warm lips sliding down over him, and he cried out at the shocking depth of pleasure that soaked through his being. His entire world was contained within this bed, within her sweet, hot mouth, within how beautifully sensual she looked doing what she was doing. He recalled thinking once before that when they made love, it was as if they were the only two people in the world, and it was like that again now. Nothing else existed.

He wanted to touch her, run his fingers through her hair, slide her body around to give her the same erotic delights she bestowed on him. More than once, he instinctively reached for her only to be reminded that he was handcuffed to the bed. She held all the control here. He remembered feeling taken by her in the limo, yet that had been nothing compared to this, the sensation now humming through his chest like lightning in a bottle. Never before had a woman seized all power over him. Never before had he imagined how damn good that could be.

When finally she rose off of him, she gazed down with those innocent eyes that made her such an alluring paradox.

"Ah, honey," he breathed, "I want to kiss you; I want to hold you."

Scrambling up to straddle him, Penny lowered short, furious kisses to his mouth as she struggled to release his wrists above. When they came free, his arms fell around her and he held her tight and whispered how beautiful she was, how perfect, and how wonderful she'd just made him feel.

She raised her eyes to his. "Make love to me on the balcony."

Ryan's stomach wrenched with the sheer volume of sexual energy she possessed, and he released a low growl in reply. "Did this just hit you, or have you...?"

"Fantasized about it," she finished for him, nodding. "About looking down on the city, feeling like I'm on the top of the world. About the breeze on my face and the stars up above and the lights at my feet, about feeling like we're part of the elements, yet still it's private, intimate, like no one exists but us."

So she felt it, too, as if they were the only two people in the universe. Since the moment he'd seen her tonight, his heart had brimmed so full he feared he might burst apart with the sheer joy of loving her. He adored what she'd done to him, the control she'd exercised over him, but now he needed to show her how *he* felt, needed to fill her with his love. And it was a love he couldn't bring himself to give voice to—not yet—but he hoped he could say it with his body.

Penny took his hand and led him out onto the small balcony, approaching the waist-high rail. Nothing stood between the high-rise building and the Ohio River but the dark night air, and walls that enclosed both sides of the balcony ensured their privacy. Her hair blew in the breeze as she peered over her shoulder at him. Her expression was both patient and beckoning, and he wished he were an artist so that he could paint the way she looked right now. He stood in awe of this glorious, sensual side of her, amazed to be the only man who had experienced it despite knowing it was an innate part of her and had been long before he'd ever climbed into that limousine.

Stepping up behind her, he brushed her hair aside to

kiss her neck, shoulder, then slid his hands around her waist, pressing his erection into the silk of her panties.

"I feel you," she whispered.

He slid himself against her and she leaned into him. He couldn't see her mouth, but reached up, grazing his fingertips over her silken lips, then let one finger dip between. It was insane, but it was as if that *other* part of himself were inside her mouth, and he moaned into her hair, then withdrew his finger and dabbed the moisture onto her nipples, knowing the light summer wind would torment them even more. She gave a sexy sigh, letting her head fall back against his chest, and he gently kneaded her breasts.

When Penny turned her head, lifting one arm behind his neck to pull him into a kiss, he slipped his hand into the front of her panties. She was wet, and if it was possible, he got even harder. She gave a hot gasp of pleasure, moving rhythmically against his fingers while his erection still rubbed her from behind.

Soon the friction was too much and Ryan couldn't wait any longer. "I have to have you," he growled into her ear, using his free hand to peel the panties to her thighs.

"Take me," she breathed.

He complied, thrusting himself into her sweet warmth as the breeze washed over them. He swore softly and she moaned. He pushed himself as deep inside her as he could, wanting fiercely to connect their bodies in a way they never had been before. She cried out with each hard stroke, meeting it with the same force. Almost light-headed with pleasure, he reached around her to grab onto the railing as they made love.

After regaining some control, he let one hand slide back down into her wetness and she eased into a more sensuous rhythm almost immediately. When her climax broke moments later, when she was crying his name in ecstasy, Ryan felt as if a warm blanket had just fallen over him. The feeling was safe and pure and made his heart overflow.

Still moving inside her, he embraced her from behind and gazed down on the shimmering river below, the headlights winding up Eastern Avenue, the dark greenery of Sawyer Point, and then he leaned near her ear. "We're making love on the top of the world, honey, just like you wanted."

Still welcoming his thrusts in breathless pleasure, her reply came in a heated whisper. "Oh, yes."

"You drive me mad," he said, and knew he couldn't keep himself from coming much longer.

It happened the very second she looked over her shoulder to say, "*You* drive *me*...wild."

RYAN LAY WATCHING Penny sleep peacefully in his arms, his soul rent with emotion.

After the brain-numbing sex on the balcony, he'd longed to tell her he loved her, yet he'd held back, confused by everything roiling in his mind. So much remained unresolved. Like where the hell Martin was, for one thing. And how to sort out this mess he'd built around his boss and Penny.

Despite what he'd kept inside, though, their lovemaking had been stupendous, and Ryan wanted more. Easing down in the bed beside her, he dropped a few smooth kisses to her silky stomach until he felt her hand move through his hair and looked up to see her eyes flutter open. He made love to her again and the world turned perfect once more.

Afterward, she laughingly smiled into his eyes, whispering, "I've always wanted to say what I said out on the balcony."

"What's that?"

Again she giggled and looked unaccountably shy. "Take me."

"I liked it," he told her lasciviously.

After a little more love talk, Penny balanced her chin on his chest and looked earnestly into his eyes. "So... maybe we should discuss things?"

Ryan sighed, then nodded. "I guess we should."

He saw her swallow nervously. "I was just wondering what will, uh, happen now? With us, I mean."

"I don't exactly have any firm answers," he admitted, "but I think we should keep seeing each other until Martin finally shows up. After all, we don't exactly seem capable of stopping anyway."

A pretty blush colored her cheeks as she smiled, but then she turned more serious again. "And when Martin *does* come back?"

He tilted his head. "We play it by ear?"

She nodded, resting her head contentedly against his chest. "A sketchy plan at best," she murmured, "but..."

"A hell of a lot better than being apart," he finished for her.

RYAN SAT in his cramped office the next day, staring at the computer screen. He was supposed to be designing Penny's menu system. Instead, he relived the previous night in his head.

Of course, that inevitably and unfortunately turned his thoughts to Martin.

Soon, realizing his concentration was shot, he left his desk and went to the lobby. He didn't want Grace to think he was a total lunatic over Martin's return, but nearly half the day had passed, and he had to know. "I guess you haven't heard from Martin again," he said, trying to sound very reasonable.

"No, not yet." Grace's voice came as light and airy as usual. "But when I do, I'll tell him how eager you are to speak to him."

Ryan tried not to seem alarmed. "Uh, no, don't do that."

Grace looked doubtful. "Why not?"

"Well, it's...nothing that can't wait until he's back. But he didn't give you any idea when he'd return?"

Grace sighed and Ryan got the idea he was getting on her nerves. Understandable, he supposed. "No, he didn't say. But as I was telling Penny last week, the man has a one-track mind—he's a workaholic. This isn't the first time he's gone away on business, then gotten side-tracked with a new client or something."

Ryan just nodded. No matter what the reason, Martin's extended absence and silence still made him question the guy's commitment to Penny.

"You know what?" he said to Grace, the idea just hitting him. "Don't order my sandwich today. I think I'll grab lunch out." He wanted to get out of the office for a while, and he also wanted to see the woman who had turned his heart on end.

When he walked into the Two Sisters Pub minutes later, it bustled with customers. Waiters and waitresses—most of them college-aged—scurried about the room from kitchen to table and back again. Spotting Penny behind the bar serving drinks, he took a stool at one end and just watched her, unnoticed. Her hair fell from the back of a Two Sisters baseball cap, and she had her T-shirt tucked into denim shorts. He smiled because not only did he love the way she looked now, but he also knew she wore some sinfully pretty bra and pair of panties underneath it all.

"These are for table three, Lisa," she said to one of the waitresses, shoving a tray of sodas across the pickup end of the bar to a tall blonde.

Then an older guy asked her for a coffee refill and she reached for the pot with a smile that lit Ryan up inside.

Penny had been happy as a lark all morning. The night she'd spent with Ryan had left her floating on air. She was in love with him and she'd been wild with him, and even though she had no idea what would happen now, nothing had ever felt more right.

"Here you go," she said, filling Mr. Bear's cup. She'd come to think of him that way after that first day he'd been in last week. He'd become a regular since then and she'd made sure to treat him with courtesy and speed to make up for her original negligence.

"So," he said, "how'd things turn out with that guy anyway?" When she gave him a confused grin, he added, "The one your sister was teasing you about last week."

Oh, *that* guy. She'd totally forgotten he'd overheard their conversation, but the question brought a smile to her face now. "Things are...coming right along."

Mr. Bear nodded pleasantly and took a sip of his coffee. He'd turned out to be quite nice, after all.

"Two beers and an iced tea, Penny," called Renee, another server, from the pickup area.

Penny turned to grab a glass and saw Ryan sitting at the end of the bar by the window, watching her. He winked. That one little wink melted deliciously down through her and she smiled at him, thinking of the previous night, which had been beyond hot, beyond magical.

She gestured for him to hang on, then filled the drink order before wiping her hands on a towel and heading down to him. "What are you doing here?" she asked, surprised but happy to see him.

"I'm here for lunch. And because I missed you."

There were moments when she thought her heart would crush beneath the weight of how much she loved him, and this was one of them. "You just saw me a few hours ago, silly," she teased.

"A few hours too *long* ago."

"Penny, I need a bowl of chicken soup," Patti called from the other end of the bar.

Darn the timing, Penny thought. She wanted the world to stop so it was just the two of them again.

"Go on," Ryan told her, seeing her frustration. "I know it's your busy time. I'll just take some of that soup myself whenever you get a chance, and a club sandwich."

"Is that it?"

His eyes turned playful. "Maybe a kiss or two if you can squeeze them in."

"Coming right up." She flashed him a flirtatious smile, then turned to Patti, in a total fog as far as the pub was concerned. "Uh, what did you need?"

"Soup. Chicken soup."

Ryan was right—she was busy, but she delivered his order a few minutes later, and popped back by whenever she had a free second. Even now, when she should be getting used to having him around, the mere sight of him had the ability to turn her inside out. And when he leaned over and whispered, "What color is your bra today?" she wanted to forget all the customers, leap across the bar, and attack him.

"That's for me to know and you to find out," she said instead.

By the time he finished eating, the rush had died down, and Penny was grateful to spend a little time talking with him. "By the way," he told her, "your new floppy drive and modem were delivered to the office this morning."

She gave a happy sigh. "It'll be nice to have my whole computer back."

"I can install the parts tomorrow night if you want."

"What's wrong with tonight?"

He grinned. "Well, tonight I have other plans for you, if you're up for it."

"I'm intrigued. Go on."

"I was thinking maybe we could do all *three* meals together today. You wanna have dinner with me at my place? Say, around five-thirty? I've barely touched any of the food we got at the grocery."

"Sounds fun."

"No. Fun," he informed her, "is what we'll have afterward, when I get to see that bra." He concluded with another wink, then rose from his stool and said, "See you tonight," on his way out the door.

She let out an enormous lovestruck sigh when he'd gone. Still smiling to herself, she reached for a rag to wipe down the bar, and caught sight of Grace watching through the window from the building's lobby.

Penny felt the blood drain from her face and knew she looked guilty as they made eye contact. How long had she been standing there? How much had she seen? Neither of them waved or smiled. This couldn't be good.

As Grace moved to the door of the pub, Penny envisioned how she and Ryan must have looked, giggling and whispering and flirting. *Please, please don't let her know what's going on.* Yet even as she wished it, she knew it was futile.

When Grace approached the bar, Penny braced herself, the ugly feeling of being caught at something ricocheting down through her. *I've just lost Ryan's job for him.*

"Hi," Penny choked out as Grace's small green eyes met hers.

Grace pushed up her glasses. "I came down to tell you Martin just called."

She'd finally heard from him herself just yesterday, of course, but for some reason, Penny couldn't have been more stunned if Grace had said the Queen Mother had phoned. "Oh?"

"He's flying back late tonight and will be in the office tomorrow morning. I figured you'd want to know."

"Of course," Penny said, absently wiping the bar and nodding. "Thanks."

With that, Grace started to leave, and Penny's heart began to lighten with the unbelievable. Maybe Grace *hadn't* seen anything and Penny had imagined all this discomfort.

Before she reached the door, though, Grace turned around. "Penny, I don't mean to stick my nose into your business, but..."

Oh no. Here it comes.

"I saw you in the park the other day."

Penny's heart sank like a brick.

"And I saw you just now, too. I don't know the whole story, and I don't have any idea what you plan to tell Martin, but...well, you might at least consider being more discreet."

Penny felt like some kind of cheating wife whose indiscretions had just been plastered across a billboard on I-75. "Grace, I'm...sorry." Her chest hurt and she had no idea what else to say.

To her surprise, Grace came back to the bar and touched Penny's hand, damp and clammy now from the rag beneath it. "I'm not the one you should apologize to."

Penny felt tears threatening because no matter what had changed inside her, she was still a nice person, still more of a good girl at heart than she'd realized, and she hated the way this looked, and the way it made her feel. She almost considered telling Grace the truth—at least about her feelings for Martin—but she didn't think it would be right. She couldn't tell Grace she wasn't marrying Martin before telling Martin himself.

As Grace turned to leave again, Penny said, "Grace, wait."

She looked back.

"I can't imagine what you must think of me right now, but it's much more complicated than you know. That's no excuse, I realize, but...well, I think of you as a friend, and I don't want that to change."

Finally, Grace's expression softened. "I think of you that way, too, Penny, and that's why I came in here. I just wanted to remind you that you're not invisible, that your actions may have repercussions."

Even after the door shut behind Grace, though, Penny still felt like a heel. Grace was right. Who knew how many people that knew both her and Martin might have seen her and Ryan just now, or some other time, like at the park or the grocery store. The world always got smaller when you were trying to keep a secret.

And now that Martin was really coming home tomorrow, and so much anticipation and buildup had gathered around his return, Penny realized just how much she didn't want to hurt him. She could try to justify her actions by reminding herself that their relationship had really amounted to nothing more than friendship, but what it came down to was that he'd fallen in love with her and had expected her fidelity for at least as long as it took to mull over his marriage proposal. She'd treated him horribly, was *still* treating him horribly. It might not feel like cheating in her heart, but how would Martin see it if he found out?

She truly did care for him. It'd been easy to forget that these past ten wonderful, horrible days, but she did. She'd known him for a long time, having shared two years of friendship before they'd started dating. Although their romance was recent, their relationship went back further, and Penny had just spent a week and a half trampling it without reverence.

Oh sure, she'd told herself she was concerned, she'd let guilt leak into her selfish pleasures, but she'd also conveniently pushed it aside time after time. Even her *guilt* had been selfish, more about her than Martin. But now, maybe for the first time since all of this had started, she really thought about *him*, the man who was her friend, the man who loved her and wanted to build a life with her, and she thought about his real feelings, as well. He would be crushed if all this came out. Of course, she still couldn't marry him, but how could she ever really be with Ryan, either, under the circumstances?

And when her thoughts shifted to Ryan, her heart caved in further. After everything he'd confided in her, about his family, his past job losses, and how important this job was to him, she'd still prodded him into bed, over and over. Again, how selfish she'd been.

After all, she'd known from the beginning that this was just about having fun. Sure, they'd had wonderful, wild times together, and sure, they'd been about as intimate as two lovers could be. He'd even sent her those panties and told her he missed her, but...it wasn't love for him. He was more worldly than Penny in the ways of sex. Well, more than she *usually* was, anyway. He'd never told her, but she knew instinctively that he'd had a lot of lovers, *casual* lovers. He knew how to flirt without going too deep, and any secrets he'd ever told her had been only because she'd pushed him with her questions. To have kept on with this relationship was selfish and thoughtless on her part. And to continue it *now* would be the most selfish act of all, wouldn't it?

For Martin *and* for Ryan.

Martin was coming back. And Grace knew their secret. How much more dire could things get? And what would happen to Ryan if he lost his job over this, over her? It wasn't just his livelihood, but his very life. And what about the money he sent home to his parents? What if he didn't have it to send anymore?

As Penny looked down at the same spot on the bar she'd been wiping for several minutes now, she realized a lot rode on her actions, so much more than her own happiness, so much more than her silly, selfish need to be wild. No matter how she looked at it, she'd spent the last ten days wreaking havoc in the lives of two men she cared for. If she stopped that now, this very minute, it might not be too late to make things right again.

WHEN PENNY GOT HOME at the end of the day, she tried to act as if it was any other day. She took off her shoes, looked at her mail, poured herself a glass of iced tea in an attempt to cool herself down. Humidity and scorching temperatures had returned, having edged steadily upward since last week's rain.

But such sadness had built inside her through the day that she knew all this pretending—even to herself—was a wasted effort. She'd made a decision, and no matter how many times she went back over it, it seemed the only right thing to do. As she'd realized during her talk with Grace, Nice Girl Penny really did remain alive and well inside her. She had to do the right thing, or she'd never be able to live with herself.

As for Martin, he'd certainly be hurt when she turned down his proposal, but not nearly as hurt as he'd be if he found out she'd taken up with someone new, his employee no less, while he was away.

And as for Ryan...well, sexual urges aside, he'd get over this quickly. It was just a matter of putting distance between them, and for more than a day or two this time. Once he refocused on his work, on the reason he'd come to Cincinnati in the first place, he'd forget about her. She'd become nothing more than a pleasant memory, a last, wild fling before he really settled down for good. And then maybe he'd even find someone else to date, someone who wasn't so wild, who wasn't so bad for him.

Penny choked back a sob at that last horrifying thought, and grabbed for the phone and dialed his number before she chickened out. Her stomach churned as she waited for him to answer.

"Hello?" His beautiful, deep voice echoed across the phone lines into her heart. How was she going to make herself do this?

"It's, uh, me."

"Hey, where are you?" He sounded happy to hear from her. "I was starting to worry."

Penny glanced at the clock; it was almost six. "I'm...not coming," she said, swallowing back the lump in her throat.

Concern invaded his voice. "What's wrong? Car trouble or something?"

"No, but I...uh, spoke with Grace this afternoon. She saw us, Ryan. In the park. And today in the pub. And Martin will be back in the office tomorrow morning."

He stayed quiet for a long, wrenching moment, so Penny rushed ahead, ready to end everything.

"So I've given it a lot of thought and I've decided we shouldn't see each other anymore."

More silence resonated through the phone until he said, "For now, you mean. Or for...?"

Her chest grew impossibly tight. "For good," she said, her heart crumbling. "I know how important your job is to you, Ryan, and I really think you'll lose it one way or another if we stay together. And I've figured out something else, too, something I've just avoided thinking about. Martin is a good man, and I've been very unfair to him in all this. I think if you and I tried to see each other, even after I turn down his proposal, I'd still always feel like I was sneaking around behind his back, committing some crime. He trusted me to be loyal to him while he was away, and I betrayed that trust with you. I can't keep doing it. For both your sakes, this is the right thing to do."

Again, silence pervaded when she finished, and it gave her the chance to go on and say everything she needed to.

"It couldn't last forever, right?" She forced a small, surprisingly convincing laugh. "I mean, it was wonderful, really wonderful, and I wouldn't trade the time we've spent together for anything. But it was just a fling. And you were probably right all along. We're in different places right now, me wanting to have fun, you being so dedicated to your work, so all in all, it's best to let it end."

She heard his heavy swallow. "What about the project? Your system?"

"Well, I was thinking maybe Patti could start working with you on it. After all, everything important is in my notes. Or maybe you could talk Martin into shifting the project to someone else for some reason. Either way, I'm confident we can get around that some way."

Silence returned once more and Penny wasn't sure what else to say. She wanted to get off the phone, end this torture. "Ryan, are you still there?"

"Yeah, I'm here." He sounded tired.

"Thank you," she said on impulse.

"For what?"

"For last week. And last night." She drew in another deep breath. "Well, I should go now. Bye."

"Penny, I—"

She hung up the phone, pretending she hadn't heard him say her name. Whatever he had to tell her, she couldn't listen to it. She had to be finished with this or she'd never get through the pain.

What now? she thought, suddenly feeling at loose ends. Her mind raced back to past relationships that had ended, and how months after a breakup, she always reached a point where she took the momentos that still remained in her life from the guy in question and threw them away. It signified the real end of things for her, the real letting go.

Biting her lip to crush her emotions, she decided she

should just go ahead and do that with Ryan now. After all, they'd been together for a week, two if you counted generously—it had been brief, so why let memories linger on? The sooner she got rid of them, the sooner her heart would be rid of him. She had a hard time trying to convince herself she wanted that, but she attempted it anyway.

Heading to her bedroom, she opened her sock drawer and drew out the red handcuffs, then walked to the wastebasket.

Yet, just as she was about to drop them inside, she stopped, hugging them tightly to her chest. The heart-shaped cuffs were a keepsake of what they'd shared, a keepsake of the love she'd let go—the love that might have been the love of her life—but she'd done the right thing, for him and for Martin. And that's what life and love were about sometimes, weren't they? Doing the right thing.

Then Penny looked down at them, a pair of red-velvet, heart-shaped handcuffs, and started laughing. What a crazy, silly, insane thing to hold on to as a keepsake!

Penny kept on laughing then, couldn't stop laughing, in fact, until she realized that somewhere along the way she'd started crying.

11

RYAN SAT IN HIS OFFICE the next morning, watching the digital clock on his desk. 8:07 flicked to 8:08. He'd come in early in order to beat Grace and so far, had avoided seeing her. However, Martin should arrive any minute now. And God only knew what would happen then. He suspected the rest of the day would be interesting, to say the least.

It was 8:09 when he thought of Penny. Wow, two whole minutes had passed without his dwelling on her. He remained as dumbfounded over her call as he'd been last night. He still couldn't believe it. One minute they were teasing and flirting and planning dinner; the next, she was not only standing him up, but giving him the boot, too.

He'd wanted to protest, to stop her, to say, If our time together was so damn special, why are you throwing it away? He'd even *started* to say something, but when she'd hung up, her feelings had been pretty clear. It was hard to believe he'd misread her so badly, but maybe she was even more complicated than he knew. Maybe she hadn't been as crazy about him as he'd thought. Maybe, as he'd feared just yesterday, this was just one big wild affair to her.

And besides, he couldn't argue with her about his job. He'd been telling himself his priorities were a mess, that maybe the job wasn't the most important thing, but just what did he think he was going to do without it? No matter how he stacked it up, his career mattered.

So he hadn't called her back. He'd let the only woman he'd ever really fallen in love with walk out of his life for a second time in a few short, agonizing days. He shook his head. Talk about a whirlwind relationship— he felt as if a tornado had just swept through his life, leaving little bits of his heart scattered everywhere.

By 8:11, his mind had drifted to the other call he'd received last night, which had also left him reeling. It hadn't been surprising to answer the phone and hear Dan's voice; after all, he'd never gotten around to returning his brother's call. But the shocking part had been when they'd started talking about Ryan's new job and his condo, and Dan had said, "You've got the life, Ryan. What I wouldn't give..."

"What?" The words simply hadn't computed in Ryan's head.

On the other end of the line, Dan had sighed. "Oh, don't get me wrong. I love Carol and the kids are great. Life is good. But sometimes I envy you, and I think about how much guts it took to leave behind everything you know and go someplace new."

Ryan hadn't known what to say, still in a state of heartbreak over Penny, yet trying to absorb his brother's words. "I...never felt I had any other choice," he finally explained. "It's what I'd always wanted."

"Well, it still takes courage," Dan said, then his voice turned uncharacteristically cynical. "Something Mom never stops reminding me."

Okay, wait just a minute here. "What are you talking about?"

Dan hesitated. "The truth is...Mom and Dad never stop singing your praises. *Ryan's doing so well in the city.*

Ryan's got such a good job. I don't know what we'd do without the money Ryan sends us. I never hear the end of it."

Ryan sat astonished for a long moment, just breathing into the phone, until finally he burst into laughter, not the least of which was due to Dan's imitation of their mother.

"What's so funny?" Dan asked.

"They do the same thing to me about you!"

The brothers had shared a good laugh and a long talk that made Ryan want to get to know Dan better, so much that he'd even invited him to bring his family to Cincinnati for a weekend sometime soon. They'd eventually concluded that their parents must be proud of both of them, just in different ways, and that they simply had the bad habit of touting each son's achievements to the other, instead of doing the opposite. All of which meant, of course, that Penny had been right, despite what he'd so strongly believed.

At 8:15, the elevator bell dinged, and lo and behold, Martin's voice finally boomed through the office.

"Hello, Grace! I'm back, as promised. Things seem awfully quiet around here—everyone have their noses to the grindstone already? They must be working too hard!"

Ryan flinched. Martin sounded a little too...enthusiastic. Not that he knew his boss very well, but the Martin who'd hired him had been much more staid and serious. Pleasant enough, but as Grace had confirmed, Martin was a workaholic and Ryan had seen that in his personality right away.

And this business about them all working too hard! What was that about?

Then it hit him. Martin had come home expecting Penny to say yes. He'd probably wheeled and dealed

Schuster Systems into a lot of business at the conference, and now he thought he was on a roll, that things would continue going his way. He thought he was getting married.

Unable to bear thinking any further about Martin's misconceptions, Ryan leaned over and nudged his office door shut. The chips would soon fall, and he didn't know where, but for now he'd just try to get some work done and hope for the best. Hell, he didn't even know what the best *was* anymore.

Ryan pulled up Penny's system on his computer and started inputting information, but his heart wasn't in the work. He continued looking at his clock as though counting down the minutes to the moment of truth. For Penny. For Martin. For him. He wondered what Penny was doing, if she was down in the pub yet, and he even considered calling her, but talked himself out of it when the phone rang.

Could it be her? He grabbed it. "Ryan Pierce."

"Ryan, it's Martin. Can I see you in my office please?" He hung up before Ryan could say anything.

Ryan glanced at the clock again. 8:28. Plenty long enough for Grace to have told Martin everything. As Ryan pushed back his chair, he heard "Taps" playing in his head. This was it, the countdown was over. He imagined reaching over to stop the clock, marking the time of his demise, but you couldn't do that with a digital, damn it.

He moved down the hallway to Martin's office, the place where all this had begun, and his chest tightened as he leaned through the open door.

"Come in, Ryan," Martin said, glancing up only slightly before returning his attention to the stack of message slips in his hand.

Ryan stepped inside and took a seat in one of the leather chairs across from his boss's desk. His soon-to-be *ex*-boss, he had a hunch.

Martin lowered the messages to his blotter with a sigh. "I've got a lot to deal with this morning," he said, "but before I do, I want to speak with you."

Ryan nodded and kept eye contact with Martin. He could feel his head being positioned in the guillotine and waited for the proverbial ax to fall.

"I know what's been going on around here," Martin said.

There it was, cutting through him in one smooth slice.

"Grace doesn't miss much," Martin went on, "and she's filled me in on everything that's happened while I was away."

"I see," Ryan mumbled.

Martin sighed. "I liked you when I hired you, Ryan. I thought you had a good head on your shoulders and you struck me as someone who knew what you wanted. You seemed dedicated to making a place for yourself here at Schuster Systems."

He paused to take a drink of coffee, and Ryan thought, Come on already. Get it over with.

"And I can see now," Martin went on, "that I made a great decision."

A large smile erupted on Martin's face as Ryan's jaw dropped. "You did?"

"Now, don't be modest. Grace told me how hard you've been working. Staying late some nights, arriving early, coming in on the weekends. And your progress report on the Two Sisters system is quite impressive. You've gotten twice as far as I'd anticipated and at this rate, we'll bring the project in way under budget, which is good, since I gave Penny a little price break." He winked. "I don't know if she mentioned it or not, but she and I are...close."

Not as close as she and I are, Ryan thought, but he just nodded like a madman and said, "She mentioned it."

"Well, anyway, I just wanted to commend you on the good work you did while I was away. I'm glad to have such a team player on board. But hey," he said, grinning and shaking a finger as Ryan got to his feet, "don't work too hard now. You know what they say about all work and no play."

Oh yeah, he knew, but no way was he going to enlighten Martin on just how much play he'd combined with work lately, or just how *not* dull his life had been in Martin's absence. "Uh, not to worry," was the only answer he could muster. "And...thanks," he added, backing toward the door.

Ryan left the corner office dumbfounded. What the hell had just happened in there? Grace hadn't told Martin about him and Penny? He almost wanted to go back and ask, just to make sure he hadn't missed something because it didn't make sense.

As he headed down the hall, he looked up to see Grace herself approaching, a stack of papers in her hand, likely heading to the copier. "Grace," he said sharply, stopping her in her tracks and meeting her eyes. Then he spoke more softly. "Thanks. For what you told Martin. And...for what you *didn't* tell him."

She didn't quite smile, but gave him a thoughtful look that at least seemed to say she didn't think he was pond scum. "I only told him the truth about your work. As for the rest, I figure that's between him and Penny."

"Well, I appreciate it."

By the time Ryan sat back down behind his own desk, though, his emotions were shifting. Sure, it was great that Grace hadn't tattled on them, and nice to know she'd noticed the good things he'd done while Martin was away, as well, but the same old issues still remained, and still stood between him and Penny.

And the more Ryan thought about it, the more he realized it had been a relief of sorts when he'd thought Martin knew the truth. Not that he wanted to lose his job. Of course he didn't. But...he just wanted Penny, damn it. He didn't want to give her up. Not for anything.

And the more he examined the past few days, the less he bought her "we're in different places right now" speech. After all, how could he have misread her need, her emotions, so drastically? Those moments when everything had stopped and she'd just clung to him said it all, didn't they? Wasn't it possible that she could be wild and want more than just that at the same time? He wasn't a hundred percent sure—he wasn't a hundred percent sure of anything today—yet he simply couldn't believe he mattered to her so little. Naturally, the confrontation with Grace yesterday had jarred her, and he could respect her concern over Martin's feelings, but he just didn't believe she was any happier about being apart than he was.

There was something he could do about this. The idea had been flirting around the edges of his mind for days, but it only materialized into something concrete just now. It was a drastic, crazy sort of notion, and he didn't even know if it was feasible, if it would work. But when he thought of spending the rest of his life without his Pretty Penny... Hell, what was the point of living if you didn't take some risks every now and then?

PENNY WAS CLEANING GLASSES as Patti took inventory of the liquor behind the bar, when the pub's door opened and Martin walked in. "Hello there, Penny," he said, his voice filled with the same bold warmth as his smile.

"H-hi." The word came out strangled. *Great start.*

She glanced at Patti, who had already put down her pencil. "I'll, uh, do some work in the office," she said, scurrying away to leave them alone.

Penny's first instinct was to remain behind the bar, maintain that comfortable distance between them, but she knew that would be cowardly. So she walked out from behind it and let Martin give her a long, rather excruciating hug before they sat down at one of the tables.

She looked into his eyes. *This is it. This is where I break the poor man's heart.* "Drink?" she asked in an automatic attempt to delay the inevitable.

He shook his head. "I have coffee upstairs. And I...really think we should talk, don't you?"

Yes, she did. So Penny took a deep breath and began, nervously. "I've been...worried. Where were you?"

"I'm so sorry, Penny," he apologized, as she'd known he would. "As I said in my phone message, time got away from me in Vegas."

"I know," she said, nodding. "You were working, learning, soaking up every bit of your conference."

Yet Martin looked uncertain. "Well, not exactly. At first, that was the case, but then..."

But then? She raised her eyebrows. "What?"

Martin took her hand and let out a sigh. "Penny, I have something to tell you."

Yet Penny couldn't suffer through the slow pace of this conversation a second longer. She'd been waiting for a week to turn down his proposal, and she had to do it now. "I have something to tell you, too, Martin," she said hurriedly, although she tried very hard to sound sad at the same time.

"No, wait." He held up one hand. "Let me go first. I need to get this off my chest."

The protest left her stunned.

"While I was in Vegas, Penny, I made a big discovery about myself."

"What's that?"

"I just don't think I'm ready to get married."

Penny's mouth fell open and her heart nearly stopped from the shock. "Oh?"

"I'm so, so sorry, Penny, but when I asked you to marry me, I'm afraid I was...on the rebound from Sheila. You remember hearing me talk about Sheila, don't you?"

Martin's old girlfriend. "Yes," she said, too bewildered to utter more.

"Well, Sheila's in software, too. She moved to Minneapolis for a job, which is why we broke up. I saw her at the conference and..."

As Penny's surprise wore off, it all started to become clear. Her heart warmed and she smiled. "You realized you couldn't live without her."

"No," Martin said.

Penny's eyes widened. "No?"

"I realized she'd held me back, turned me into a real stick-in-the-mud." Martin's eyes glazed over slightly. "She made us wear matching Christmas sweaters, Penny! It seemed fine at the time because I was in love, but no more." She'd never heard him sound more vehement. "What I discovered in Vegas after sharing a buffet with her and then, on the way back to my hotel, chancing to meet a lovely showgirl named Cherise is, I haven't yet lived."

Penny felt numb. "You haven't?"

"Cherise changed the way I look at life. We painted the town red, and lost a thousand dollars at roulette!"

He laughed and Penny gasped.

"We danced the night away in nightclubs!"

Penny gasped again because she'd seen Martin dance and it wasn't pretty.

"We drove out into the desert and made passionate—" He stopped, his face reddening. "Oh, Penny, I'm so sorry." He shook his head in distress. "Look at me. I came home wanting to break this to you gently and instead I just spew it all out like the volcano at the Mirage. Have you seen it, by the way?"

Penny remained nonplussed. "On TV."

"Quite a sight, especially after a few shots of tequila, let me tell you." He stopped again, shaking his head once more, as if clearing it. "What it comes down to, Penny, is..."

She gently tilted her head as her shock slowly gave way to a different sort of understanding this time, one that hit a little closer to home. "You've discovered you have a wild side," she said softly.

Martin nodded and turned somber. "I'm sorry. I hope you're not too hurt."

"Actually, Martin, I...think it's for the best."

Martin's expression brightened, clearly surprised at how easy this had been, since he'd expected to leave her heartbroken. "Well, thank you for being so understanding. I hope we can still be friends."

"Of course." She sealed the promise with a smile.

"And maybe occasionally take in an exhibit at the art museum together?"

"If you won't find it too tame," she teased.

He winked and got to his feet, and Penny followed

suit, then he reached to squeeze her hand once more. He had just turned to go when he stopped and looked back. "I can't believe I'm so rude. What was it you wanted to tell me?"

Penny shook her head. "Nothing."

"Are you sure?" He leaned forward slightly, as if prodding her.

"Yes, Martin. I'm sure."

"Well then," he said slowly, "I'll see you soon." He headed toward the door, leaving her standing in the pub alone.

She stared after him for a long moment, still trying to absorb all he'd just told her, and realizing what probably would've happened if Martin had gotten her note that day and joined her in the limo. Thank goodness *Cherise* had been the one to uncover *his* wild side.

Finally, she let out a laugh, but it dissipated quickly into thoughts of Ryan. She was so happy that he had been the man to get in that car with her, and that she'd had the last week and a half with him.

She'd almost considered stopping Martin on his way out, confessing about her and Ryan. Considering this new change in him, he might've thought it was fine. And the horrible guilt she'd been suffering on Martin's behalf had suddenly dissolved into nothing. But she hadn't told him the truth because she still didn't really know how he would take it, and what if she were wrong and it made him angry, or hurt? She still couldn't risk Ryan's job that way. And yet, maybe, just maybe, there was hope now for her and Ryan to share a future together?

But no. Depression whisked through her, quickly squelching the hope.

She kept forgetting one important thing. Ryan didn't

love her. When all was said and done, the dreaded F-word kept reentering Penny's head—*fling*. That's what their relationship was, what it had always been. There had never been any question about that except maybe in her own lovestruck mind.

Just then, the office door squeaked open a crack, and one of Patti's eyes peered through.

"It's safe," Penny said. "He's gone."

Her sister yanked open the door. "Well? How'd he take it? Tell me everything. Spare no detail."

"You won't believe it."

"Try me," Patti said. "You've shocked me so much lately that it would take quite a whopper to throw me at this point."

"Well, you'd better sit down."

RYAN LINGERED in the shadow of a potted ficus tree in the lobby outside the Two Sisters Pub, watching as Martin exited. He'd been on his way to see Penny, to tell her his crazy idea, when he'd realized Martin had beat him to her. Now he started casually toward the pub again, passing Martin on the way.

"Hey there, Ryan, scouting for a little breakfast?"

The guy still seemed awfully happy for someone who'd just been dumped.

Unless—oh God—he *hadn't* been. The thought nearly paralyzed Ryan, but he hid his reaction. "Uh, yeah."

"Great Danishes at Penny's place." Martin pointed, then winked at Ryan for the second time in half an hour. "She gets a fresh tray from the bakery across the street every morning."

Martin moved on toward the elevators, and Ryan picked up his pace until he practically burst through the pub's door. Penny and her sister sat at one of the tables, and both looked up, clearly stunned to see him barreling into their restaurant.

Patti sighed. "I'll be in the back," she said, then rose to make her way to the office.

Ryan wasted no time striding to the table, staring down at the woman he loved. "Did you tell him you wouldn't marry him? Did you?"

"Not exactly, but—"

It was just as he'd feared. "Penny, you can't marry him! You don't love him! And he didn't even call you for over a week! I won't let you throw away your whole—"

"Wait!" she interrupted, getting to her feet. "If you'd let me finish, you'd know the only reason I didn't tell him was because he told me he doesn't want to marry me first."

The news nearly knocked the wind out of Ryan. "Is he nuts?"

"Well, he *did* seem a bit out of sorts, but—"

"Listen, I have something to say and I can't go slow or I might start thinking I'm crazy and stop."

She stared at him, her pretty eyes wide upon him. "Well then, go ahead."

"I'm gonna quit my job and start my own company," he announced.

She looked confused. "Why?"

He thought the answer was obvious. "So I can be with you. So we can do wild things if we want to and it won't be anyone else's business. And because..." he spoke more softly now "...I can't sleep nights without you."

He saw her pull in a deep breath and thought, *Please tell me you want me, too.*

"Is this," she began uncertainly, "what you really want?"

"To start my own company?" he replied. "Well...not exactly. I mean, I like where I am. I like the work I'm doing for Martin and I already know he values it. I think I could go places at Schuster, grow with the company." Then he bent one finger to lift her chin, and gazed into those warm blue eyes that had the power to swallow him. "But do I want to be with you? Definitely. Otherwise, I'd never even consider this."

Penny's heart constricted. She couldn't believe Ryan would make that kind of sacrifice, take that kind of risk, for her. She'd never been more touched by any gesture in her life, but she couldn't let him do something like that if his whole heart wasn't in it. She pressed her hands to his chest. "Ryan, it might not be necessary to take such drastic steps for us to be together."

"What do you mean?"

"Didn't you hear what I said about Martin? He doesn't want to marry me. And when he was out in Vegas, he wasn't just working."

"What was he doing?"

Penny smiled into Ryan's eyes and spoke softly. "He was finding his wild side."

Ryan blinked. "You're kidding."

"He met a showgirl. Cherise."

"Cherise?"

"I think they had sex in the desert. And drank a lot of tequila."

Ryan raised his eyebrows in disbelief. "Way to go, Marty." Then his eyes took on the sexy look she loved. "And you know, that sounds like something you and I should try."

She laughed. "The desert or the tequila?"

"Nothing against a good shot of tequila, but I was definitely talking about the desert."

She smiled her agreement, leaning in to lift a slow, sweet kiss to his lips. "I didn't tell Martin about us," she went on. "I still didn't know how he might feel about it. And I couldn't risk your job that way without discussing it with you first. But maybe what I did while he was away, and what you and I choose to do now, won't matter anymore. Maybe if we told him the truth, he would understand."

Ryan had the same feeling even before she had spoken, and he knew what he had to do. He supposed the answer had been dangling in front of him all along, but he'd been too afraid to reach out and grab it.

"I'll be back in a few minutes," he told Penny.

She raised her eyebrows. "You're going to do this now, tell him this very minute? I mean, shouldn't we talk about this first, plan what to say?"

"Just trust me," he said.

FIVE MINUTES LATER, Ryan stood before Martin's desk. He wasn't going to beat around the bush. He'd waffled on this for too long in the first place and was ready to take action. He needed to clear the air and quit keeping secrets. He needed to be the sort of man Penny deserved. "Martin, I have something to tell you."

His boss smiled, and it finally occurred to Ryan what Martin was *really* smiling about. Cherise in the desert. "What's that?" Martin asked.

"I don't know how else to say this, so I'll just say it. While you were away, I fell in love with Penny."

Martin quit smiling and leaned forward in his chair, as if he couldn't quite fathom what he'd just heard.

"I realize I was overstepping," Ryan went on, "but it

was...bigger than the both of us. I never really knew what it meant when people said that, but now I do. I tried not to want her, but—" he shook his head "—I can't help it. I can't stop it. So...is there any chance this is okay with you or, all things considered, should I just go clean out my desk?"

Martin tilted his head. "Let me get this straight. While I was away, you fell in love with Penny."

"Yeah." Ryan nodded.

Martin leaned farther over his desk. "*My* Penny."

"That's the one."

"So you're saying while *I* was out in Vegas, *you* were here, romancing the woman I had just proposed to?"

To say the very least, Ryan thought. But he kept it simple. "Yep."

Ryan tensed as Martin slowly bent his head in the other direction, then flashed a smile so bold it made Ryan flinch. "Well, that's the best damn news I've heard all day! Other than her not hating me for withdrawing my proposal, that is. It killed me to hurt her like that—she's a tenderhearted woman, you know."

"I know."

"And she's...well, she's very conservative. Very innocent. Pure at heart."

Ryan held in his smile and simply nodded.

"So nothing would please me more than to see Penny with a stand-up guy like you, Ryan. I hope you'll make her very happy."

Oh yeah, Ryan thought. *I'll make her happy, all right.*

PENNY HAD SPENT the last half hour trying to absorb all that happened this morning; heck, in the whole past two weeks. Martin didn't love her, and had likely never loved her—he'd merely been on the rebound. And

Ryan really cared for her. Enough to risk the career that was so precious to him, and so important to his family. Of course, she'd also spent the time worrying about Martin's reaction and praying Ryan's career remained intact. It was difficult to start a business—she knew that from experience—and she wanted Ryan to be happy with his decision. So much remained at stake; her heart turned somersaults in her chest.

She'd just finished updating Patti when the pub's door flew open and Penny almost dropped a beer mug. Her eyes desperately searched Ryan's as he headed toward her.

Patti pivoted toward the door that led to the street. "I'll go take a walk."

Penny smiled her apology, then shifted her attention back to Ryan, biting her lip as he neared the bar. "Well?"

"He's glad," Ryan said, smiling. "He gives us his blessing. Although it wouldn't have mattered. Either way, I'd be down here right now telling you I love you."

He loved her? A happiness like none she'd ever known stormed through Penny's veins. She couldn't breathe, her emotions becoming some bizarre mixture of confusion and an elation beyond measure. "But I thought—I thought this was just a fling. I thought you couldn't fall in love that fast. Remember, you told me that once."

He took her hands and gazed into her eyes. "I was wrong. And I was a fool to think anything was more important than the way I want you." Her whole body went warm as he pulled her into his embrace. "So, tell me, do you have any other fantasies we haven't explored yet?"

Penny raised her eyebrows. "I do, in fact."

"Don't keep me in suspense."

"Well...I've always kind of wanted to do it here, on the bar."

Ryan peered at the mahogany, then glanced over her shoulder toward the street. "Kind of risky with all these plate-glass windows. Are you ready to go that far?"

Penny didn't answer, but her body flared with a familiar desire as she slid her arms around his neck and plundered his warm mouth with her tongue. Their bodies pressed together, thighs intertwining, and she'd just begun to lose herself in the sweet friction when Ryan whispered breathlessly in her ear.

"I, uh, hate to break it to you, but even *I'm* not that wild." He gazed past her again, first toward the street, then to the pub's office. "We should look into getting some big shades for these windows, but for now, honey, we'll have to make do in there."

At the moment, Penny hardly cared where they did it, as long as she had her way with him, now. A slow smile spread across her face as she realized she finally had what she'd always dreamed of—the kind of passion that was too urgent to wait. Grabbing Ryan's tie, she led him into the office and shut the door.

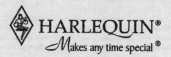

This Mother's Day Give Your Mom ✿ A Royal Treat ✿

Win a fabulous one-week vacation in Puerto Rico for you and your mother at the luxurious Inter-Continental San Juan Resort & Casino. The prize includes round trip airfare for two, breakfast daily and a mother and daughter day of beauty at the beachfront hotel's spa.

INTER·CONTINENTAL
San Juan
RESORT & CASINO

Here's all you have to do:

Tell us in 100 words or less how your mother helped with the romance in your life. It may be a story about your engagement, wedding or those boyfriends when you were a teenager or any other romantic advice from your mother. The entry will be judged based on its originality, emotionally compelling nature and sincerity. See official rules on following page.

Send your entry to:
Mother's Day Contest

In Canada
P.O. Box 637
Fort Erie, Ontario
L2A 5X3

In U.S.A.
P.O. Box 9076
3010 Walden Ave.
Buffalo, NY
14269-9076

Or enter online at www.eHarlequin.com

All entries must be postmarked by April 1, 2002.
Winner will be announced May 1, 2002. Contest open to
Canadian and U.S. residents who are 18 years of age and older.
No purchase necessary to enter. Void where prohibited.

PRROY

HARLEQUIN MOTHER'S DAY CONTEST 2216
OFFICIAL RULES
NO PURCHASE NECESSARY TO ENTER

Two ways to enter:

• **Via The Internet:** Log on to the Harlequin romance website (www.eHarlequin.com) anytime beginning 12:01 a.m. E.S.T., January 1, 2002 through 11:59 p.m. E.S.T., April 1, 2002 and follow the directions displayed on-line to enter your name, address (including zip code), e-mail address and in 100 words or fewer, describe how your mother helped with the romance in your life.

• **Via Mail:** Handprint (or type) on an 8 1/2" x 11" plain piece of paper, your name, address (including zip code) and e-mail address (if you have one), and in 100 words or fewer, describe how your mother helped with the romance in your life. Mail your entry via first-class mail to: Harlequin Mother's Day Contest 2216, (in the U.S.) P.O. Box 9076, Buffalo, NY 14269-9076; (in Canada) P.O. Box 637, Fort Erie, Ontario, Canada L2A 5X3.

For eligibility, entries must be submitted either through a completed Internet transmission or postmarked no later than 11:59 p.m. E.S.T., April 1, 2002 (mail-in entries must be received by April 9, 2002). Limit one entry per person, household address and e-mail address. On-line and/or mailed entries received from persons residing in geographic areas in which entry is not permissible will be disqualified.

Entries will be judged by a panel of judges, consisting of members of the Harlequin editorial, marketing and public relations staff using the following criteria:
- Originality - 50%
- Emotional Appeal - 25%
- Sincerity - 25%

In the event of a tie, duplicate prizes will be awarded. Decisions of the judges are final.

Prize: A 6-night/7-day stay for two at the Inter-Continental San Juan Resort & Casino, including round-trip coach air transportation from gateway airport nearest winner's home (approximate retail value: $4,000). Prize includes breakfast daily and a mother and daughter day of beauty at the beachfront hotel's spa. Prize consists of only those items listed as part of the prize. Prize is valued in U.S. currency.

All entries become the property of Torstar Corp. and will not be returned. No responsibility is assumed for lost, late, illegible, incomplete, inaccurate, non-delivered or misdirected mail or misdirected e-mail, for technical, hardware or software failures of any kind, lost or unavailable network connections, or failed, incomplete, garbled or delayed computer transmission or any human error which may occur in the receipt or processing of the entries in this Contest.

Contest open only to residents of the U.S. (except Colorado) and Canada, who are 18 years of age or older and is void wherever prohibited by law; all applicable laws and regulations apply. Any litigation within the Province of Quebec respecting the conduct or organization of a publicity contest may be submitted to the Régie des alcools, des courses et des jeux for a ruling. Any litigation respecting the awarding of a prize may be submitted to the Régie des alcools, des courses et des jeux only for the purpose of helping the parties reach a settlement. Employees and immediate family members of Torstar Corp. and D.L. Blair, Inc., their affiliates, subsidiaries and all other agencies, entities and persons connected with the use, marketing or conduct of this Contest are not eligible to enter. Taxes on prize are the sole responsibility of winner. Acceptance of any prize offered constitutes permission to use winner's name, photograph or other likeness for the purposes of advertising, trade and promotion on behalf of Torstar Corp., its affiliates and subsidiaries without further compensation to the winner, unless prohibited by law.

Winner will be determined no later than April 15, 2002 and be notified by mail. Winner will be required to sign and return an Affidavit of Eligibility form within 15 days after winner notification. Non-compliance within that time period may result in disqualification and an alternate winner may be selected. Winner of trip must execute a Release of Liability prior to ticketing and must possess required travel documents (e.g. Passport, photo ID) where applicable. Travel must be completed within 12 months of selection and is subject to traveling companion completing and returning a Release of Liability prior to travel; and hotel and flight accommodations availability. Certain restrictions and blackout dates may apply. No substitution of prize permitted by winner. Torstar Corp. and D.L. Blair, Inc., their parents, affiliates, and subsidiaries are not responsible for errors in printing or electronic presentation of Contest, or entries. In the event of printing or other errors which may result in unintended prize values or duplication of prizes, all affected entries shall be null and void. If for any reason the Internet portion of the Contest is not capable of running as planned, including infection by computer virus, bugs, tampering, unauthorized intervention, fraud, technical failures, or any other causes beyond the control of Torstar Corp. which corrupt or affect the administration, secrecy, fairness, integrity or proper conduct of the Contest, Torstar Corp. reserves the right, at its sole discretion, to disqualify any individual who tampers with the entry process and to cancel, terminate, modify or suspend the Contest or the Internet portion thereof. In the event the Internet portion must be terminated a notice will be posted on the website and all entries received prior to termination will be judged in accordance with these rules. In the event of a dispute regarding an on-line entry, the entry will be deemed submitted by the authorized holder of the e-mail account submitted at the time of entry. Authorized account holder is defined as the natural person who is assigned to an e-mail address by an Internet access provider, on-line service provider or other organization that is responsible for arranging e-mail address for the domain associated with the submitted e-mail address. Torstar Corp. and/or D.L. Blair Inc. assumes no responsibility for any computer injury or damage related to or resulting from accessing and/or downloading any sweepstakes material. Rules are subject to any requirements/limitations imposed by the FCC. Purchase or acceptance of a product offer does not improve your chances of winning.

For winner's name (available after May 1, 2002), send a self-addressed, stamped envelope to: Harlequin Mother's Day Contest Winners 2216, P.O. Box 4200 Blair, NE 68009-4200 or you may access the www.eHarlequin.com Web site through June 3, 2002.

Contest sponsored by Torstar Corp., P.O. Box 9042, Buffalo, NY 14269-9042.

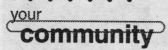